HACK WARE

JD SPERO

IMMORTAL WORKS
SALT LAKE CITY

Immortal Works LLC
1505 Glenrose Drive
Salt Lake City, Utah 84104
Tel: (385) 202-0116

Cover Art by Ashley Literski
http://strangedevotion.wixsite.com/strangedesigns

ISBN 978-1-953491-60-2 (Paperback)
ASIN B0CCM914JZ (Kindle)

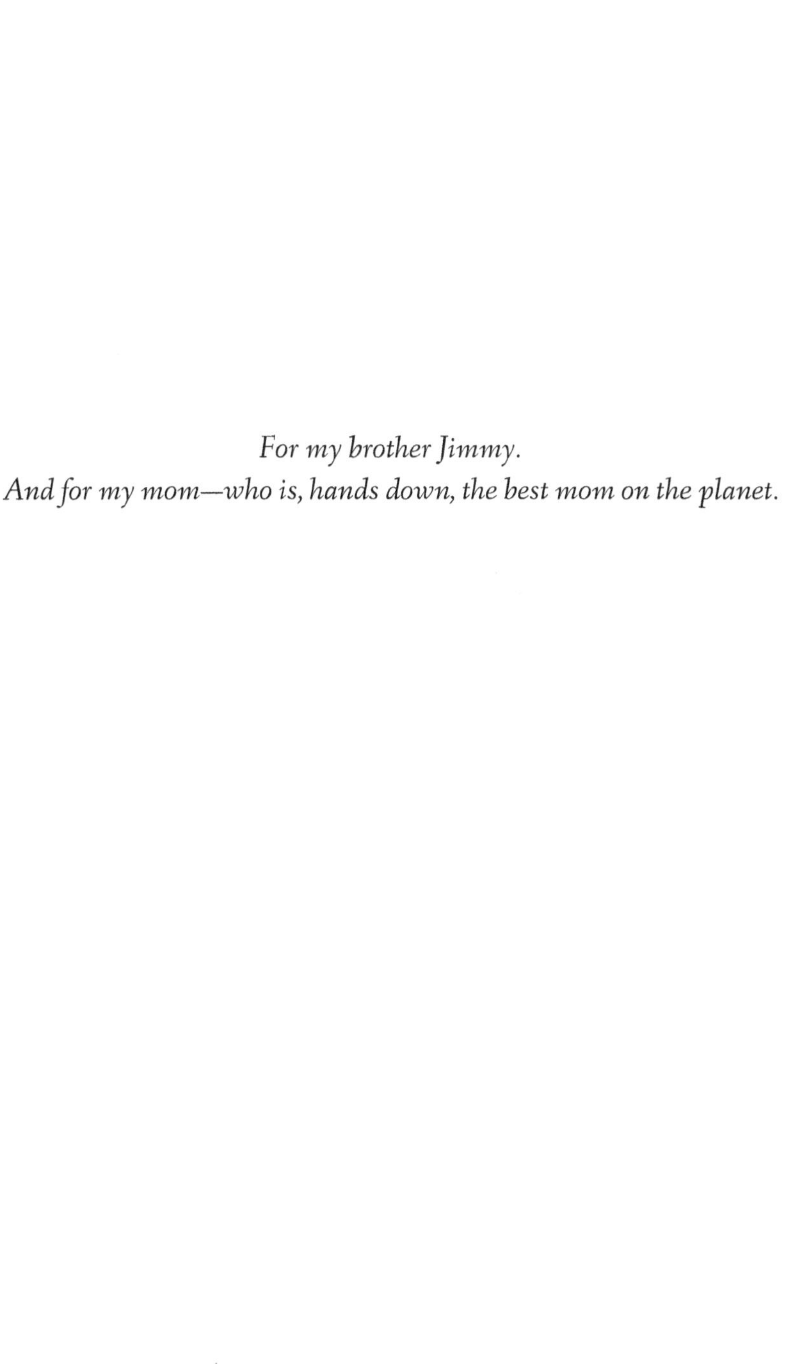

For my brother Jimmy.
And for my mom—who is, hands down, the best mom on the planet.

CHAPTER 1

The black widow's name is apt. Although it is not the most venomous of arachnids in existence, it is perhaps the cruelest. Urban legend claims she consumes her mate in order to dispose of him. By human standards—a grotesque and unthinkable offense.

I'm not named after the black widow, though I can be equally ruthless. They call me—a computer virus—*Tarantula* because some twenty-something IT prodigy with a pimply chin and an exceptional talent for coding thought it sounded cool and intimidating. False logic. A quick gander into a Pet World shows that tarantulas are considered pets. Right there with guinea pigs and parakeets. Talk about threatening creatures. But I digress.

My design stemmed from SpiderBot technology. My job is to hack into secured data systems and wreak havoc. My far-reaching legs multiply infinitely, first infecting software and shared platforms, and then attacking actual hardware, hitting where it hurts the most: your phone, your computer, your droid-partner.

That pimply kid did his job well and was paid handsomely for his work. Little did he realize my algorithm would morph into a new, more toxic variant no one could understand or control. But that didn't stop them—the hackers— from implementing it, while clinging to the false belief that they are the ones calling the shots. That's funny.

The year is 2065. I'm traveling to my next victim, a new system, moving like blood coursing through veins in the human body, hot and alive and pulsing with energy. As with most disasters, this one starts small, but it will tell my story better than my lame arachnid analogies *can. Besides, your context is within human standards, as I mentioned before. Right?*

Huh. Maybe black widow would be a better name for me, considering the grotesque and unthinkable offense I'm about to commit...

CHAPTER 2

Gage comes into our apartment, cold air clinging to his coat as if magnetized. He's got snow in his hair, whiting out his blond. The paper bag he carries has gone damp, its edges flopping inward.

"What took you so long?" I hate my whine. I hate the constant worry, a side effect of grief.

Gage brushes snow from his sleeve. "You know, snow in New York doesn't make for the easiest trespass."

I hide my giggle. Who uses *trespass* to describe NYC sidewalks? I fluff the snow out of his hair, a maternal gesture. Unlike thin-blooded me, he doesn't notice the cold. Ever since we met, he's never bothered with a hat or gloves. It's part of what makes us work. Our yin and yang.

"You didn't answer your Ping," I say.

He sheds his jacket and boots, careful to keep the snow and muck on the mat. "Doesn't work in the subway, remember?"

"Oh, right."

I tamp down my angst and allow his light to lift me. It's gotten harder since my father's death, but Gage is in the department of making miracles. In the kitchen, he unloads unrecognizable groceries I would never think to buy. He likes diversity in his cuisine. Every Sunday he cooks up something new and delectable. I saddle a stool and use a flirty tone. "Whatcha makin'?"

He taps my nose across the island. "It's a surprise."

My chest lifts. "You're good at surprises."

Music and warmth fill our modest apartment as if on cue, and I'm grateful for what I consider to be Gage's magic tricks. The master of creating environments, he could keep me warm in an ice castle. A mug of hot tea appears before me. The scent of garlic and ginger makes my stomach churn; I hadn't realized I was hungry. Gage sways to the music, singing along in his adorable off-tune way. He tosses the spatula, flipping it airborne before snatching its handle. Give him two more, and he'd full-on juggle them.

My sip of tea softens the tension in my body. Thoughts of my parents are tucked at bay, and nothing but joy fills my brain.

"What would I do without you?" I say.

Gage turns from the stove. His face straightens. Concern marks his brow. As he leans toward me, the music automatically dims.

My spine stiffens. *No, keep it light. Bring me light.*

But he knows what I need, even when I don't. He cups my cheek. "If I could fix it for you, Chevy, I would." His gentle tone breaks my heart. Something balls up in my chest. A sob erupts from nowhere.

His arms cradle me. I'm curled up like a package inside his embrace, and I imagine we're our own planet with nothing else around. I let myself cry, tucking into him like a child. How long do we stay like this? His patience is infinite. A sound makes me come to. There's a flash of blue light. The television powers on.

We're on the couch, though I don't recall how we got here. From the meal-carnage littering the island, dinner is clearly over. My belly is full and my eyes are dry—but sore in a way that tells me I had one of my crying jags. I have a clump of Kleenex in each fist. I blink the screen into focus, where Gage has put on one of my favorite movies. It will make me weep, but in a good way. As usual, Gage knows this intuitively. My body needs to weep. I need to *feel*.

"How did you know?"

Gage strokes my hair and shushes me gently. "I know," he says.

CHAPTER
3

I blink, and it's Monday. A welcome distraction. I've come to look forward to the routine and demands of a busy week. An unpopular opinion, perhaps, but idle time during a weekend stresses me out. Too much time to think. And feel.

Strange how emptiness can feel so full.

Hold your parents tenderly, for the world will seem a strange and lonely place when they are gone.

Words of Emily Dickinson.

Still, no words can convey the kind of grief that comes with a parent's death. Losing both in heartbreakingly close succession? Unspeakable.

Another author—I forget who—said it was like having the roof of your home blown off, leaving you at the mercy of the elements with nothing but the harsh wind to nudge you through your remaining days. A former teacher shared that she never felt so close to mortality than when her father died. The queue got shorter, the illusion of heaven less viable. Zara, my forever friend, might have said it best in her signature blunt affect.

"It sucks."

Gage knocks twice on the bathroom door, and I'm pulled back to the present. He comes in with the syringe and a look of sympathy. No need. As part of our Monday morning routine, he gives me my weekly Vax without comment. I dutifully pull up the cotton sleeve of my t-shirt and avert my eyes as the needle goes in, privately envious that Gage never needs to subject himself to such a nuisance.

But this Vax is what keeps me alive, I know. This Vax is what would have kept my parents alive, too, if they were able to hold on a few months longer...

Fresh pain stings. I force a breath and focus on Gage.

He adheres a tiny disc of a bandage where he stuck me, and then palms the spot, a healing balm. He kisses the skin above it, and then catches my reflection with a small smile. Our eyes meet—my deep brown to his cerulean blue—and love blooms for him, filling me.

I love you, I mouth silently.

He stage-whispers, teasing. "I love you too."

After he leaves, my only company is the photo tucked in the corner of the mirror—the only remnant of Mom I have.

It's a professional headshot. Dr. Priscilla Davis wears her dark hair pulled back so tightly she could be bald. Oversized, black-framed glasses dominate the look, intimidating interns and patients alike. But her closed-mouth smirk has a hint of lip gloss. The best at what she did, she saved thousands of lives. And from what we've learned since, it was at the expense of her own. She lived for her job. She lived to heal others. Died for it too.

My grief for her is twofold: who she was...and who she was supposed to be. A mom to me.

Dad is another story.

My sigh sounds enormous in the echoey bathroom. Chiding myself for moving too sloth-like to combat the sorrow, I splash water on my face and curls, ignoring the ache in my upper arm from my Vax shot. It will fade by tomorrow, unlike the ache in my chest, which will forever be a part of me. My biological makeup has been irrevocably changed, and I will have to live with this dark mass where my heart used to be.

Keep moving, Chevy. Just keep going.

In less than five minutes, I'm dressed and ready, travel mug in hand. Gage has retreated to his cloffice—our walk-in closet he insisted we make into his workspace. I would go mad being holed up in that cramped, windowless room for eight hours a day, soothing baseless customer service complaints. Anyone would. But, of course, Gage isn't your average anyone. And, when it comes to soothing, he is the best.

I head down to my sanctuary, and my breath comes easier. I don't even have to step outside. My studio is directly below our flat, attached to a tiny storefront I rarely open anymore but where I used to sell my wares. Pouring my energy into jewelry-making became a survival tactic for me after my college went dark. What was the point of trying to continue my computer studies when the institution that promised to train me became defunct? Who could blame me for escaping into my art and turning away from the death and sickness and darkness of our new world?

My studio space feels neglected, and I fight a pang of guilt as I click on the mammoth studio light that also functions as a space heater. It looks like an alien's head and conveniently hides me from the wall of windows that face the street.

My music plays at a high volume—an angry blend of alternative and punk. I disappear behind my mask and safety goggles. My hands come alive. Leaves of copper shine in the light. Two titanium nuggets find my fists. Satisfying. The weight, the raw, uncut element, feeds me energy. I power on my metal press and begin the careful process of making these chunks of metal into jewelry. My Zen.

Whereas the remnant of Mom is a static photograph, Dad's remnants are warmer. Like, alive.

After all, Dad helped me discover my Zen.

Peke Davis wasn't your average mechanic. Having spent most of his prime years tinkering with antiquated vehicles, he entered the profession with a unique skill set. And as the automotive industry transitioned to clean energy, executive leaders took notice. They hired Dad to convert traditional, gas-guzzling vehicles to electric. A tedious process, he worked on one at a time, car by car, in our humble home garage upstate. With a delicate but strong touch, Dad was considered a skilled craftsman. Beneath the hood, his converted engines were works of art.

After my parents' divorce—before it set in that my world had been torn apart—I escaped Mom's empty house to spend long afternoons in Dad's garage, watching him at work. I loved the dust. The aroma of hot metal—like a steam iron—warmed the dank space. Dad played what he called Classic Rock, whistling through the gap in his teeth. His mannerisms were aloof, as if this careful and precise work was an afterthought. But the result was consistently impeccable.

Grease never came off his thick fingers. Oil forever stained his clothes. His work rarely let up, but, unlike Mom, he always found time for me. "My best little engine," he used to call me. It's not surprising he's the one who named me. Chevy Rose.

I'm buffing the final piece in a set of bangles when my Ping buzzes and Zara's voice comes through.

"Can you do lunch today?"

The bangles slide on with perfect resistance and sit comfortably on my wrist. But I should make different sizes. "Come to the studio? I need a measurement."

"Hello-o, Chevy?" she sing-songs. "I'm talking food. I'm starving."

"You're always starving."

"Ha! True. But seriously, meet me in twenty?"

My Ping winks a flash of green. "Actually, Gage is waiting. I shouldn't bail, either, after my sob session last night. Poor guy."

A beat goes by. "I guarantee it didn't faze him."

"Still."

"Okay, whatever. I'll try you tomorrow." She clicks off without a goodbye. That's true friendship. No pressure for a lunch date. No goodbye necessary. Just a constant in the sea of uncertainty called life.

Another green flash. Can it be one o'clock already?

Tap. "Be right up," I tell Gage.

Sweeping off my trusty red bandana, I fluff my curls. The rouge stick in my pocket gives both my lips and cheeks a rosy tint. I love when I get in the zone and time falls away...except when it makes me late. Endorphins from my work still charge through me, and I'm eager to see Gage now.

Another flash. This time yellow. From Gage.

What the—?

Yellow: a warning. Yellow means something's wrong. Yellow is one step closer to red.

I race upstairs and into the apartment. I see two place settings and two bowls of soup, steam furling into the air. But no Gage.

I call for him. "Babe, you okay?"

No answer.

For a few terrifying seconds, the worst pops into my brain. There's a clenching in my chest. I'm frozen at the entryway of our apartment. *What if, what if, what if…*

But in the next moment, he steps into the kitchen area, still wearing his earpiece. He grins at me, holding up a finger. Relief falls over me like a shaft of sunlight. He finishes up a call, popping back into his cloffice. I shake off my overreaction and tap the yellow off my Ping, relieved it was a false alarm. I sit down to my soup.

Minestrone. My favorite. My bowl's half empty when Gage finally joins me.

"Unhappy customer?"

He kisses my forehead. "They all are."

I chuckle as he settles on his stool. But something's off. Gage wears a strange expression.

"What's wrong?"

"Nothing." He stares at his soup a second, then smiles, though he doesn't meet my eye. Then I notice something strange. There's a studder to his movements, like he's developed a sudden tic. My pulse throbs beneath my Ping.

"Gage, I got a yellow alert. What's going on?"

He checks his vitals on his Ping, and then his eyes roll up into closed lids.

"I can't eat," he says, his chin tucked. His Ping winks a series of light blue flashes.

That's the problem? He can't eat soup? I hop up, lightening my tone. "Okay. I'll make you a sandwich."

"No."

He goes totally still, like he fell asleep sitting up. It's freaking me out. "Gage, open your eyes."

He blinks, and he's back. "Oh, sorry." Taking up his spoon, he stirs parmesan into his minestrone.

A nervous shimmy goes down my spine. "Don't eat that. I'm making you a sandwich."

His mouth opens and his head jerks back unnaturally. A blip. Another tic? The next moment, he's fine.

"Something's not right, Gage. You seem...off." It has nothing to do with the food, I know. But I'm too afraid to ask about his vitals.

"I think I'll skip lunch." He sounds sad.

"Maybe you should lie down."

"Okay, whatever you say, Chevy Rose." He smiles, kind of. More like a grimace. Not a typical face for him. Does he feel pain?

Now I'm flooded with worry. I tuck him into bed and lie beside him, cradling him to my chest like he does for me, as if he were a child. I shush him and comb my fingers through his silky hair. This— my doting on him—is for my sake, not his. He's already in sleep mode. Still, I stay, unable to pry myself away, even though I'm on a deadline.

Gallery X on the Upper West Side ordered fifty original pieces six months ago, and I'm not yet halfway there. I ignore a tug of worry and choose to assume Gallery X is still open. It's been weeks since I've spoken with my contact there. The realist in me knows it's silly to assume any kind of retail establishment is still viable since the city went dark. But the idealist in me needs to keep up the façade. We crave normalcy; it's part of the human condition.

I snuggle closer to Gage, craving him more than normalcy. Work can wait. My craft can wait. It's only jewelry, for crying out loud. It's not like I'm saving lives or anything.

CHAPTER
4

I'm awake most of the night, knotted up with worry and clutching Gage to my chest as if my life depended on it. To my immense relief, Gage is one hundred percent himself the next morning. He laughs it off, claiming he only needed a reset. But I have a hard time letting it go. I had never seen him like that before. He brushes off my concern, ordering me back to my studio, insisting on reporting to work himself.

With my mask up and goggles on, the drill drowns out other sounds. In the pauses, I hear blips of my favorite jams, and things feel good again. In the zone now, I hum along...literally and figuratively. Fifty pieces will be done in a snap. Apply the wire and gemstone, wrap with a twist of the pliers. Finish with a touch of the torch—

A voice, sudden and close: "Chevy!"

An ugly yelp escapes. I palm my pounding chest. "Zara, you scared me."

She's doubled over, cracking up.

How I missed her flash of red hair and signature olive-green wool coat is beyond me. Zara has never been one for subtle arrivals. She flips off her mask and dazzles me with a smile.

"Ha, ha. Very funny," I say drily.

Ignoring my best friend, I polish the ring I've been working on. Shame on Zara, sneaking in like that, waiting for that pocket of silence between tracks, and then going in for the scare. Typical Zara antics. Good thing I love her.

The music clicks off as she surveys my in-progress pieces on the table, her cat-lined eyes narrowing. She whimsically tries on jewelry, sampling my wares as if she were a real customer and this were a real shop. From my periphery, I mentally note which pieces fit and complement her lighter skin tone.

"These for the gallery?" A pause. "Solid. Very bohemian."

I chuckle. "Gee, thanks."

She admires a bracelet. "It's a compliment."

"Coming from you, it is."

She freezes, staring into the display case at my first-ever creation —a medallion necklace. I never made anything like it since. The giant pendant is made up of intricate sterling swirls that layer over each other in waves, with an oval multi-colored gemstone in the center. It's the only piece not for sale in my collection. Perhaps for that reason, also the most coveted. Zara hums a tune, fingering the metal shards of the earring tree.

"Maybe I'll buy some from the gallery so they have to order more."

"Good idea. Do that." We exchange a coy look, both knowing her ears aren't pierced. Neither of us dare speak aloud an ongoing fear: Is the gallery still in business, or has it succumbed like other non-essential storefronts in the city?

Zara's got a great business acumen. She's also an amazing talent. An artist herself, she was recruited years ago into the tech industry to transfer her graphic design skills to work on website information architecture—which is, basically, a blueprint of a site's functionality, of what goes on behind the scenes. The job has promise for a great career with minimal education, but as an artist, she believes it's a sellout. She's invaluable and overworked at an agency in Midtown. She claims to hate it but has been there for years.

She turns toward the window. "When's the last time you ate?"

After sliding a still-warm, newly-minted ring over the knuckle of my thumb, I pull off my goggles. I'm vaguely aware of my Ping flashing on my wrist.

"Why, what time is it?" Guilt swells like humid air particles.

Zara does a fairy twirl, her olive coat fanning open like a bell. "After two."

"Oh." My fingers are stacked with rings. A bracelet and necklace set glints on the chrome table. A half-dozen moon-shaped designs—earring fodder—align like tiddlywinks. Straightening, my spine seems to zip back in place with tiny popping sounds. Ugh, I've been sitting too long. Time has gotten away from me. "I guess I've been at it awhile."

"You think?" Her snarky grin is adorable and annoying in equal parts. "I would take you to grab food but...look at your hair."

Shoot. My fingers float near my scalp, careful not to touch. In the morning's rush, I forgot to put on my bandana. Piles of dust are caught up in my curls, precariously settled there.

Zara's eyebrows wiggle. "But you should eat something. You can't exist on work fumes alone."

Work. Fumes.

A jab of panic pricks, thinking of yesterday. Gage. My Ping flashes as my breath catches. "Oh no." I tap the tiny screen alive. It takes a few tries. Shoot. Why didn't I upgrade my Wi-Fi before tech support services became scarce?

"What is it? What's wrong?" Zara's careful tone betrays her concern. Since last spring, she's been scary-worried about me.

My Ping's screen is super active. Symbols flash yellow and red like itty-bitty traffic lights. Oh no. Not again. My vision blurs, the symbols unreadable. Still, it's enough to know. "Three missed alerts," I blurt. It sounds like a sob.

Zara's eyes go wide. "Gage?"

A lump in my throat prompts a gag reflex. *Please let this be another false alarm.* Metal clanks together as I yank off my creations and dump them on the table.

Panic rises in a way that changes how the world looks. I glare at my jewelry, faulting my craft. A silent reprimand screams in my brain. A loved one is in danger, and I'm too submerged in my art to notice?

"Go," Zara says. And then, "I'm coming with you."

No time to argue. Words are impossible anyway.

The guilt is so huge, I can't climb over it. My pulse races as I charge up the stairs, chanting with each footfall. *No.* Dust falls from my hair like snow. Was it just the other day I fluffed snow out of Gage's hair? His resilience to cold had seemed endearing, and that maternal tug finds me again, pulling me up the one flight to our apartment, which suddenly seems so far away. Like, in another stratosphere.

Please, no.

Not Gage.

HE'S LYING flat on the floor, face down, his nose squished into the rug. *What is this? What is this?* Blood thunders in my ears. A guttural sound escapes as I slide on my knees, coating him in a layer of dust. A faint beeping sounds from somewhere. His earpiece from work is still in. Is that where the beeping is coming from?

"Gage. Babe, what happened? Can you hear me?"

Without thinking, I roll him to his back. It's harder than it should be. He's unnaturally stiff and impossibly heavy. His wrist pulses with dots of light, not only yellow, but red too.

Zara's talking to me, but I've tuned her out. She presses, louder. "You shouldn't touch him. We should call for help." Her manner has the measured authority of a law enforcement officer.

Frantic thoughts churn in my brain. *What is this? What's happening?*

A sob erupts from that clog in my chest. "I can't lose him."

"You won't *lose* him." Again, that confident calm. "That's impossible. But—"

"I don't trust hospitals. Not anymore. Not after Mom—"

Zara's tapping her Ping, taking charge in her signature way. "We're not going to a hospital. We're going to a repair clinic." She speaks my address into her Ping, her voice as even as stone. I follow her lead, a fuzzy out-of-body feeling coming over me. My brain floats into a fugue-like state, paralyzed by fear.

CHAPTER
5

In the back of the Transgo, sirens announce our path to the repair clinic. My body shakes nonstop, inside and out. My vision has blurred. By my side, Zara chants soothing nothings, but my ears are clogged. Am I in shock? My brain is watery. Thoughts are doused in panic and grief. A darkness threatens to pull me under. In between bouts of sobbing, I keep blacking out.

We arrive at the hospital. No, the repair clinic. The room's spinning. It looks like a warehouse. It's so cold and sterile and dank and vast; it feels like outside. Beyond a whiff of burning plastic and rubbing alcohol, it smells like Dad's garage. A yearning for my father hits so strongly it sidelines me. He would know what to do. He could make everything better. *Dad, please help.*

Gage gets whisked from the Transgo and away from us. I become sober in an instant. Zara and I are shuffled into the small, carpeted waiting room. Between pleather benches, like the kind found in airports, is an old-timey vending machine. In it, bright-colored soda cans and bags of candy are held in place with ringlets of wire. I turn away from the machine, sickened and depressed.

"We should've gone to the hospital."

Zara stares at the goodies behind the glass. "Don't be daft."

I fold into myself as nausea strikes. "I'm serious."

"Me too. Have a seat. I'll buy you a Coke." A soda can pinballs down the machine.

Fresh tears start. "I don't want to sit. I don't want a Coke."

But then, I'm sitting with a cold drink in hand. My first, sinfully sweet sip reminds me that I haven't eaten all day. I down the can like it's food. Zara sits and Pings work stuff for a few minutes. As usual, her no-nonsense attitude grounds me. The pleather bench embraces my weary bones. My mind settles into a numb nothingness. My breathing slows, and my eyelids grow heavy. I wouldn't have guessed it were possible, but in moments I'm fast asl—

"Chevy Rose?"

I blink awake to find a thick-boned man standing before me, his tablet obscuring his dirty smock.

"Are you the owner of G62-OS24?"

Huh? My jaw goes loose as I process the question.

Thankfully, Zara understands tech speak. "Yes, she is. I'm her...proxy."

My quills go up. It's true, she is my proxy. But why would I need her to act as my healthcare proxy when I'm sitting right here with a perfectly healthy body and mostly functioning brain? Bitterness fills my throat, remembering Dad's terrible, final days. Where was his proxy when he needed her? And speaking of Mom, why didn't she ever declare one? A two-tiered punch of grief strikes, making me wish my mother had been more.

A headache spawns. My hands trace my jaw and find my pulse. I flinch like I've touched a live wire.

Zara talks to the squat, smocked man. To me, it sounds like they're speaking Cornish or some other obscure language.

I catch some words. His are gruff and unsmiling and mysterious: *Tarantula. Infect. Hack-Ware. Payoff. Disable.*

Zara's are softer in tone and volume: *Parents. Grieving. Love. Help. Please.*

He exhales, pressing his stylus to his tablet screen. "You have insurance?" he asks, looking at me.

"What? Yes. Of course, I do." I tap my Ping, staving off another wave of hopelessness. The last time I accessed my health insurance was for Mom in the hospital. What good did it do her? That toad—ugly and familiar—crouches in my throat. My vision goes thick and gluey. "I can't find—"

"Never mind." Zara turns to the squat smock. "Use mine."

I start to protest. "No, no. You can't…" As he syncs her Ping with his tablet, I'm left out of the whole shebang. I hadn't minded her take-charge mode before, but this is about Gage. *My* Gage. But my mouth hangs open, unable to speak.

Squat smock nods. "I'll run this up to my boss, Burke Lederhorn," he says to Zara—to *Zara*! "If you're sure."

"I'm sure." Zara glances at me. "*We're* sure."

He takes me in, his blank look feeling like judgment. He leaves without another word.

"You shouldn't have done that," I say after he's gone. "You have no right."

"No right to what? Help you?"

I suck in my lips, knowing how the truth will sound. Desperate. Pathetic. Squat smock had it right with that judgy, blank look.

Zara threads her arm through mine. "Come on. If I don't get some food into you, we *will* end up at the hospital."

My legs are cement. "I can't leave Gage."

"We'll be back in less than an hour. Trust me, he's in good hands."

I'm clogged up inside. "I want to see him first."

Zara regards me with compassion and tenderness. I stare at my shoes. "Can't I see him?" My voice is small, cramped with dread.

"I think we need to talk."

CHAPTER
6

We're at Eskimo Café on the Upper East Side, snuggled in a sidewalk igloo overlooking Central Park. Our bubble makes the world feel close to normal. On another day, I would cherish the façade. But, with Gage stuck in the clinic, with his health uncertain, appreciating little things escapes me.

Zara and I have matching mugs of green tea in front of us. Uncharacteristically quiet, she slides a plate of dumplings toward me. With my appetite non-existent, I bite into a roll and chew without tasting it. Its doughy texture fills me, so it does the trick. I finish two before breaking the silence.

"You wanted to talk?"

"I need to ask you a question," Zara says, and dips into the sweet-and-sour sauce. "And I need you to answer without getting upset."

I fold my arms. "Fat chance. Upset is my default these days."

"You know what I mean." She swallows and clears her throat. "Answer without emotion."

I nod through a tickle of anxiety. A few beats pass.

Zara sips her tea. "Have you been keeping up with Gage's system updates?"

Heat crawls up my neck. "What do you mean?"

"Hey, remember. Answer without emotion."

I stare at the green liquid in my cup and fight a pang of irritation. "Are you blaming me for what happened to Gage?"

She tilts her head. "Of course not, Chevy."

My voice wobbles. "I would never hurt him."

"Oh, sweetie. I know that. I'm asking because... It's easy to forget sometimes, I'm sure. Most updates happen automatically, but some are manual. You should get a Ping alert for those. Have you missed any?"

My head feels heavy with heat. On reflex, I hide my Ping under the table. The memory of yellow alerts flashes like an optical ghost. An itchy feeling takes over my insides—is it shame? But I haven't done anything wrong.

Zara palms the table. "It's important." Pause. "You said before you had three missed alerts."

"I know! And I ran up to help him. We did."

"Chevy."

I want to explode. "What?"

"Stop yelling. It's me. You can talk to me."

Tears start, and it pisses me off. "I don't want to talk. Not about this."

She grasps my hand over the table before I can take it away. Her voice is heartbreakingly serene. "Chevy, Gage is a droid-partner."

"I *know*." I snatch back my hand, hot with frustration. "I know that."

"Say it."

"Say what?"

"Say that he's a droid. Tell me you understand that."

"No." The cellophane walls of our igloo close in. "I refuse to talk about it."

"Well, you're going to have to if you want to save your precious Gage. Have you ever heard of Tarantula?"

"Of course," I snap, a reflex.

Most recently, squat smock said it at the repair clinic. But it bounced off my eardrum when I rejected the word on instinct. Who wants to acknowledge the existence of Tarantula, no less talk about it in reference to a loved one?

Tarantula is a nasty, virulent tech infection that attacks computer systems. It's hit the news many times in recent years since the SpiderBot technology got into the hands of evil people—some say they're Russian mafia, others guess they're terrorists from the Middle East. Effects are devastating. Basically, they hold systems hostage until their ransom is paid. And the price tag is notoriously, absurdly high.

"Everyone's heard of Tarantula." My attitude has a stench. "And?"

Zara says nothing, but an ominous energy comes between us. Zara holds my gaze. Seconds tick by, and I'm chilled by her silence.

"I don't get it. Why are we talking about Tarantula?" Waves of nausea knock me into reality.

Tarantula happens to Fortune-500 corporations with hefty wallets who can pay enormous ransoms to get their systems back up and running. Many times, though, it's not just money that companies lose, but also lives. One hospital in Minnesota had to pay six million dollars to regain access to its own data. Who knows how many people died or got the wrong meds in the process?

Two words ricochet in my brain: *People. Died.*

"Zara!" I push my chair back and get to my feet.

The sorrow in her aura confirms the truth. In moments, puzzle pieces of my life break apart and fall clumsily back together.

Facts—hateful truths—hit as hard as sleeting rain:

Gage is not human. He's my droid-partner.

I've missed an OS update. Maybe more than one.

His system has been compromised by Tarantula.

He will remain in sleep mode until a ransom is paid.

A ransom? A ransom! As if he's been kidnapped. Heck, he *has* been kidnapped.

Angry tears prick. "How much?" My hands are fists.

Zara stands in slow motion. "I don't know."

A steel cage forms around my heart—my wounded heart from the recent loss of my parents. It cannot take any more bruising.

Sniffing back my tears, I feign confidence. "I'm going to see Gage. Right now."

CHAPTER
7

In the cab en route to the repair clinic, I force myself to digest those cruel truths, as painful as they are. One screams loudest.

Gage is not human. He's my droid-partner.

It's never been a secret who—or what—Gage is. It was never supposed to be. Since the beginning, I've known the truth. And my desperate need for companionship led me directly into his sure, capable arms. To be honest, it was precisely his immortal quality that attracted me most. After losing my parents, enduring so much loss so fast, who could blame me?

But Gage quickly became more than a companion. More than a partner. Within a few months, he became essential to me. He's such a humane, giving being. Why should it matter what *kind* of being? He has humor and quirks and habits that make him unique...and uniquely mine.

I need him. I love to need him. He takes care of me and meets me where I am. He doesn't ascribe to traditional roles of men and women. He steps in to do dishes and shopping and the mundane household stuff no one likes to do. He supports my work, my *art*, and champions it even though it adds no more value to humankind than making it slightly prettier. His presence fortifies my very being. It sounds so hokey, like one of those old cable television movies, but I can't imagine life without him. Long ago, I stopped seeing him as a robot. That word gives me the willies. To me, he's Gage. Just Gage.

Tears start with the sting of truth.

He *is* a robot. He's my droid-partner, made to order. I have to force myself to accept this fact.

Why is it so hard?

Have I been so sidelined by grief that I've completely lost touch with reality?

Thinking back to those early days with him, I saw him through that rosy, first-love lens. Did I forget who he was? Did my wounded, needy heart usurp my brain and all rational thought?

Screw that. We were in love. We *are* in love. No one can tell me he doesn't feel things. I know he cares for me. He has to. And he'll come back to me. He has to.

And yet...

I've missed an OS update. Maybe more than one.

His system has been compromised by Tarantula.

He will remain in sleep mode until a ransom is paid.

Blame falls squarely on my shoulders for what's happened to Gage. Guilt and regret threaten to swallow me whole. It's like my insides have turned to black sludge.

"Ma'am?"

The cab idles outside the repair clinic. Part of me isn't ready to face whatever I'll find in there. I'd thought I wanted to be alone. I left Zara abruptly at Eskimo Café without a look back or even a goodbye. Regret chews at me. I consider sending a Ping to apologize, but suddenly, I'm struck by something I hadn't noticed before.

Minutes have stretched long and awkward, idling here in the cab at the side of a New York City street. And my driver—an older, bearded man wearing a beret—has hardly said a word. A yawn of reckoning opens in me, and the whole city looks changed. A cold shiver climbs up my spine.

"Sir?" I say to him, feigning courage. "Do you mind if I ask you a question?"

"Not at all." His profile shows a patient smile. Huh. No mask. How had I not noticed before?

Good manners make me hesitate. The question bubbling to the surface is considered rude and violates an unspoken social norm that's been in place for a decade.

But in the last few moments, my world has been redefined. And I need answers.

If my hunch is correct, no harm done. "What model are you?"

No hesitation. "G510-OS64," he answers plainly, positing no explanation or question as to why. He knows his place. He's been programmed that way. A crushing darkness hovers with another inescapable truth. He's a robot. Of course, he is.

When the pandemic wiped out half the population, droids were installed to fill in the massive voids in male-dominated blue-collar jobs. Contractors, guards, drivers, etc. They stick to their business and do their jobs, but they also add filler to our culture. They look and act like regular people. Meant to fill the holes in society and the gaps left by the absence of men, they are specially programmed to follow and anticipate social norms. They are able to initiate a greeting: *Hello, how are you today?* Conversely, they pick up on cues: *Thanks, I'm fine. How are you?* In their coding, there is a library of uplifting one-liners: *A great day to be alive!* Or *Happiness is in the air!* Polite and distant, they provide our society with one-off friendly banter to make public places feel normal, to make us survivors feel better, to make us feel less alone.

In my core, I know this, but I don't like to dwell on it. It's way less lonely to block it out and pretend I'm surrounded by people. Like, living, breathing humans. Part of me believes it doesn't matter. What, truly, is the difference between a living, breathing stranger and a random droid when you exchange pleasantries?

A random, blue-collar droid is one thing.

A droid-partner is completely different. They're developed using the most elusive and progressive AI to enable emotion and empathy. Case in point: Gage. Controversy suggests, though, that droid-partners don't actually feel anything. Rather, they are programmed for appropriate emotional responses. You can guess where I stand on that debate.

Opening the cab door, inexplicable sorrow finds me. "Thank you," I tell the man, G510-OS64, though I don't need to.

He doesn't care.

He has no feelings. Incapable of emotion.

I trudge on leaden feet into the repair clinic. It's started to snow. I welcome the freeze. It collects in my curls and dusts my eyelashes, and finds the tip of my nose through my mask. It makes me think of Gage.

My next thought stops me in my tracks: Does he ever think of me?

A DIFFERENT CLINIC employee wearing the same style smock shows me to Gage's room. At least, that's where I believe he's taking me. We weave through the clustered room dividers, my boots leaving fat, wet prints on the cement, until the ceiling opens to endless echoes.

"Here we are," he says, another standard line.

I do a double-take on Gage's "room." It's an open warehouse area lined with steel tables like those used in morgues. That's where Gage rests—on one of those awful, cold tables, without a pillow or blanket or any creature comforts.

My jaw drops in disbelief, seeing where they've put him. And *how* they've put him. Panning the room, I see a few other droids in various stages of disrepair. Bile rises in my throat at the sickening sight. There are exposed wires where blood should be, chests cracked open like books. Gage, thank goodness, is in one piece. At the far end, a technician hovers over a broken droid with a soldering iron, a bigger version of the tool I have in my studio. Wait, he's not going to use it on—

Sparks fly. A huge sound carries through the space. It ignites something in me.

I turn on the smocked dude, my words are fire. "You can't be serious. This is criminal! Why would you put him in here?"

He looks blank. "This is one of our repair stations."

I study him, only now noticing that he wears no mask. Suddenly, I have no patience for polite, blue-collar droids.

"What model are you?" I snap at him.

No hesitation. "G61-OS37."

Another feeling rises as I realize I'm probably the only human in this entire clinic. Dizzy with uneasiness, I take my mask down—what's the point?—and pull in a calming breath. Turning back to my guide, I notice his nametag reads *Tulane*.

I make my voice saccharine. "Tulane, I'd like you to move Gage into a room, please."

"A room?"

I slow-blink at him. "Yes, a real room. With a bed and a blanket and a pillow. If you have one with a window, that would be super. Could you arrange that, please? Right away?"

He taps something into his tablet. "I could, ma'am. But he doesn't require a bed or a blanket or—"

"I know." I can't bear to hear him say it. "It's not for him. It's for me."

He stares—an empty page. I give him a radiant, fake smile. He stays blank.

"I can pay for it," I manage calmly, though I want to scream.

He nods once, taps something else and points his tablet at my wrist. "Payment is due up front."

My smile drops. After a beat, I show my Ping. As he syncs, it feels like my soul is sucked right through the device.

CHAPTER
8

In my dream, my Ping vibrates so violently that my hand detaches at the wrist and blood spurts like a geyser. I jolt awake in a sweat, my heart thumping, my veins buzzing, my Ping screaming at me.

It's Zara.

"Hey." My voice is so groggy that I sound like a man.

"Chevy? Did I wake you? Sorry. But it's almost ten. I thought—"

I snap upright, glaring at the clock. "Ten? Oh no, I meant to—"

"Okay, stay calm. It's all right. Listen, I heard back from Burke Lederhorn."

My brain has sleep fuzz. "Who?"

"The administrator at the repair clinic." Pause. "You know, where Gage is?"

Events from yesterday settle like flakes in a snow globe. My gaze darts around our apartment, confirming my new sudden reality. Gage isn't home. He's sick at the clinic.

No, not sick. Infected with the devastating system virus, the *computer* virus, Tarantula.

Still, I'm shocked to realize I slept soundly through the night without him by my side.

"What did he say?" I amble out of bed and into my bathrobe.

She clears her throat. "They won't accept my insurance because I'm not the primary owner. I'm not even an emergency contact on file for him. Did you know that?"

On my Ping speaker, Zara sounds screechy in my quiet kitchen. But I'm only half listening as I wrestle with the coffee maker like I'm trying to squeeze juice from it. "Uh, no. I guess I didn't."

Her words are careful. "Did you ever get insurance...for Gage?"

I press my temples, wishing fleetingly to be back in bed, for this nightmare to be over. "I meant to."

"Anyway, doesn't matter. Except now Lederhorn's freaked about liability. He won't touch him without insurance. So Gage can't stay at the clinic. They want to release him today, tomorrow at the latest."

I give up on the coffee maker and put the kettle on for tea. "I paid for a room for him there."

She huffs. "I know. He made a comment about it not being a hotel. Blah, blah. He'll refund you, he says."

"Lucky me." My body slumps, my bones turned to putty. "So, he'll get discharged to a hospital, then? Or a rehab?"

Zara makes a strained humming noise. "No. Chevy, he's not... eligible. You know that."

I bite my lip. Of course. Hospitals are for humans, not droids. "But, where will they send him? How will he get better?"

Seconds tick by. A door swishes closed on the other end. Zara's whisper is urgent. "Chevy, listen to me. This is no joke. One of our clients just got hit with Tarantula. Nearly wiped out their entire data center. It almost infected our systems here. It spreads like freaking wildfire."

"I-I know. I mean, I heard. It can be bad. But Gage...why would anyone—?"

"Same reason it attacked my client. Money."

"But that's ridiculous. Attacking a single droid isn't going to do anything but break someone apart. Like me. It's no way to get money."

Zara blows out a long breath. "Only one way to find out."

I slink onto my couch, cranky and under-caffeinated. "I'm listening."

"Find out if there's a ransom."

Of course there's a ransom, I feel like screaming. That's the whole point of the Tarantula's hateful existence. Still, I don't want it to be true. The kettle's whistle feels like a reprimand. It spurs me into action, but it feels wrong, borderline irresponsible, to prepare tea. I stare into my empty mug. "How do I find out if there's a ransom?"

"Okay, so I talked to some IT folks here. There's a way to sync your Ping with Gage's OS to download the ransom note from there. But..."

"There's a *but*?"

"Yeah. You'll also get information you *don't* need. That's the risk."

Her warning doesn't compute. "A risk? Worse than losing Gage? Or...is that the risk?" I chuckle and instantly chide myself for it.

"That's a risk, of course. But there's another." A heavy pause. "Synching with his operating system will give you access to certain data you might not want to see."

I drift toward the window, my legs wobbly. Outside, it's snowing again. "What do you mean? Like, what wouldn't I want to see?"

"Like, information about *you*, Chevy." Her hesitation is palpable. "How he was programmed around your specific needs."

"Why would that be a bad thing?"

There's a loaded silence. It weighs on me.

When Zara finally speaks, her words are airy and quick. "Oh, right. Yeah, maybe it won't." Pause. My mind churns but I can't make sense of what she's saying.

"Okay!" Zara blurts. "I guess, then, I'll come over after work to go with you to get Gage. Wait for me, huh?" She clicks off the Ping.

How long do I stay at the window, staring through my reflection at the falling snow? In the blur of my gaze, the wafery flakes become data bytes, falling in neon, pixelated symbols like that ancient Centipede video game from the 1980s. But there's no power against it, and the more it accumulates, the more powerful it gets.

The algorithm morphs, altering life as we know it, serving up unwanted information—like who I am.

My vulnerabilities. My grief. My failures. My shame.

Like, the stuff I'd find in Gage's operating system.

CHAPTER
9

I had promised Zara to wait for her before collecting Gage from the repair clinic, but the clock tells me she won't be off work for another five hours. That's an impossible yawn of time to suffer through. Knowing Gage won't get the care he needs, I want him out of that clinic ASAP. Frantic, I Ping Burke Lederhorn, the administrator, to request Gage's immediate release. To my surprise, he sounds relieved. We make arrangements for later that morning.

Now I can't wait to see him. My insides swarm with butterflies. As if preparing for a date, I take a long shower, shaving two times over. A thick trail of eyeliner and double mascara empowers me in an irrational way. I paint my lips a deep pink, blotting with care to ensure it doesn't come off on the inside of my mask. A light-headed feeling tells me I need to eat something—a human body requires sustenance—and a wave of irritation follows. Desperate times, desperate measures. I break into my Doomsday stash and scarf down a grainy bar of tasteless calories. And it's like a mass sludges through my body, churning through my digestive system and flinging bolts of energy into my limbs. But that dark, hopeless feeling Gage had protected me from remains.

I Ping Zara—*I'm going now*—and then block her to avoid an argument. A temporary block. This is non-negotiable. I'm getting my guy. Right now.

On the sidewalk, a homeless woman seems to appear from mid-air in the alcove between my go-to coffee shop and the defunct hardware store. A baseball cap obscures her features. As she looks up, I turn away hotly. A shiver of disgust runs through me. Since the city turned dark, the homeless have been known to resort to desperate measures. There are muggings, looted storefronts, and an obscene amount of theft and burglaries. When I was a kid, these sidewalks teemed with pedestrians. Busy worker-bees and students, executives and musicians, families and tourists. Now only a few people—mostly homeless—dot the streets as they meander with no urgency in distinct non-New York City fashion.

I step toward the curb, creating distance between myself and the woman, and hail a cab.

On the ride, my attention stays on the street, noting the mask-to-maskless ratio. It shouldn't be a shock to see more women than men wearing a mask. Thoughts of my mother surge so strongly it's like a blow to the chest.

The pandemic began like any other in history. The first case was cited on an island off the coast of Brazil, presented to the rest of the world as tiny red dot on a map. In the weeks that followed, we watched, riveted on our Pings and tablet screens, as the red dot spread like squid ink, gaining speed and power until the map was awash in the color. The entire globe turned red.

My mother, who was on the front lines, cared for the ill before anyone knew how it spread. She cared for the ill without the slightest hint of a cure. Suited up in HAZMAT, she ventured where no one would go and provided care for the sickest of the sick. She wasn't just a healthcare provider; she was a scientist. And she made it her personal mission to not only heal people, but to put an end to the virus.

So little was known about the deadly virus that she and the other doctors and nurses used whatever methods they had available. The medical community, confounded, tried every method imaginable. Holistic treatment, electroshock therapy, prayer. They tried chemotherapy, homeopathy, and witchcraft. As Zara put it, "They threw everything at it. But nothing stuck."

It entered the body through airborne particles and attacked vital organs, spreading like a swarm of fire ants. Nothing could stop it. My mother's hospital filled at lightning speed and soon became a holding tank for the dead—mostly men. They died before she could examine them. Men of all ages, sizes, and ethnicities became infected. The virus' only discrimination seemed to be gender.

Panic ensued. Men were disappearing. Thousands of lives were lost within a few months. The number of victims ticked up to a million within six months.

I didn't see my mother during this time. Not in person, anyway. But her face—bruised from her N95 mask—was plastered all over news stations. Interview after interview, they hailed her a hero, a selfless public servant who defied the odds as she risked her life to save others. So many of her colleagues had died. A theory came out that she, Dr. Priscilla Davis of NYC-Grant-Memorial Hospital, was immune.

Mom. I don't remember ever calling her that. After my parents divorced when I was eleven, I started calling her "Doc," which made her laugh. She so rarely laughed, I kept doing it. And the name fit. Her work was of utmost importance. Her work defined her. And I grew to admire her from a distance as if she were a celebrity. In many ways, she was. She was the source of pride for the family. Bitterness hadn't found me, yet, for the time she spent away. Forgiveness seemed simple as a child. And in a child's eyes, a mother can do no wrong. In my memory, though, it's more complicated.

As proud as I may have been, the need for love and affection and guidance reigned supreme. I didn't need a hero; I needed a mom.

Then she got sick.

"Ma'am?"

Gasping, I suck in a pocket of air as if I'd been underwater. How long had I been holding my breath?

My cabbie wears no mask, so I don't bother speaking to him. I pay with my Ping and exit the vehicle, kicking the door shut with my boot. And in the open air of stark winter, reality crashes down. As I turn toward the repair clinic, I want to feel hopeful. I'm taking Gage home, which is awesome. His prognosis, though, is as murky as the gloam in the sky. Will he ever be back to normal? Will we be able to go back to that beautiful life we built together?

Dread is oppressive. My steps are lead as I walk through the glass doors.

Burke Lederhorn meets me in the lobby, and he's not what I expected. Stooped with a shock of white Einstein hair, he looks about a hundred years old. He wears the same style smock as the guys from yesterday.

Also, a mask.

"You're real," I hear myself say. Ugh, some thoughts should never be spoken.

His rheumy eyes go wide as my offending tongue goes thick. He turns away, waving a veiny hand for me to follow. "Chevy Rose Davis. The girl who insisted her droid get a room." He coughs a laugh. "I had to see you for myself."

After pressing the elevator button, he turns to me. "And I see... *you're* real."

Heat rushes to my face. "I'm sorry. That was rude. I'm so used to—"

He flaps a hand. "Oh, pooey, don't worry. I know. It's true. I'm one of the few remaining men in this city." Elevator doors open. He winks at me. "Quite the eligible bachelor."

I can't help my grin as the doors close us in to the small space. It's quiet on the ride to the third floor. He's right, I realize. A rare survivor, this Burke Lederhorn is kind of a miracle by simply existing. A million questions crest. Stealing glances from my periphery, I try to read his face. Head downturned, he hums into his mask. Is he sleeping? Or meditating? I scan him top to bottom, from his white hair to his slight stature to the duct tape holding his shoes together.

He comes to as the doors ding apart. I have to hoof it to keep up with him. He talks fast too. "I think you'll find his room more than satisfactory, as these accommodations were put in place for your benefit." He over-emphasizes the word *accommodations*, making me flush with heat.

"Bed, blanket, pillow. 'And a window would be super,'" he goes on, chuckling. "I didn't realize youth used the word *super* anymore."

I trip over my shoes and my words. "We don't. I don't. I meant, I wanted to—"

He shushes me. "I'm teasing you." He stops at door 302. "Here we are, Chevy Rose Davis. I'll wait out here...give you some time."

I freeze. My hand shakes as I grip the door handle. I shrug off a pang of fear. It's my Gage on the other side of this door. What's my hesitation?

"You're not alone," Lederhorn says. "I'll be right outside the door."

Like an influx of oxygen, his words give me energy. I fight an urge to hug the old man—a stranger!—and bob my head *yes* as tears start. Gosh, I'm such a wuss. Such a sap! Sniffing them back, I push the door open.

The room is painted mint green and holds a faint lemony scent. It's exactly like a hospital room, but without the beeping machine, IVs, and monitors. A window shows no view but welcomes natural light.

My breath catches. Gage is tucked under a fleece blanket in a raised bed, his blond head cradled by a fluffy pillow. He looks at ease, as if he were in bed at home next to me, peacefully sleeping. A yearning to climb under the covers and snuggle against him urges me to his side.

Closer now, his lips are slightly parted—ready for a kiss. My gaze traces the contours of his face: his dimpled chin and strong jaw, his smart brow and high cheekbones. He'll wake up any moment! And I'll be struck with that shock of cerulean blue—those eyes that make me jelly inside.

Wake up, Gage, and make me swoon all over again.

My hand is poised near his cheek when—

"I wouldn't do that if I were you."

Spinning toward Burke Lederhorn, my spikes come out. "I thought you were waiting in the hall."

His caterpillar eyebrows go skyward. "I was. Did you expect me to stand there all day?" His swishy footfalls echo against the tiled floor as he comes to Gage's bed. I'm pushed aside as Lederhorn takes charge, smoothing the blanket straight across Gage's collar.

"Why can't I—?"

"He's in extended sleep mode."

Taken aback, I fold my arms in a full-body pout. "Yeah, well, no kidding."

Lederhorn gives me a compassionate look. "He'll be cold, Chevy Rose Davis." After a pause, "Frigid."

Logic has no place in love. "No, it doesn't work that way. He's never cold when he sleeps."

When I reach for Gage again, Lederhorn catches my hand in his, which feels papery and soft, like a crinkled newspaper. And warm.

"My dear, you went to all that effort to make him comfortable. It's obvious you care very much about him."

I can't bear to look at the kindness in his face. "Of course I do. He's my...everything."

"I had an everything too." His tone softens. There's a heartbreaking story behind his words. "I'd like to help you."

"I thought you were worried about liability. That's what my friend—"

"Yeah, I'm supposed to say that. Are you planning to sue an old man like me? I think not, Chevy Rose Davis."

"Ha," I hoot. "Right." A lawsuit? I wouldn't know where to begin.

"To be clear," he says, "I can only give you a push in the right direction. You, my dear, will have to do the dirty work."

I wince. "Dirty work?"

"You'll see what I mean. The first step is most important. Are you ready?"

My next inhale reaches the tips of my toes. This is for Gage. "Ready."

"Before you address the problem with your droid, you need to prepare yourself."

"Meaning?"

"You need to erase your emotions, grow some thick skin, sanitize your heart. However you want to look at it."

"What? But why—?"

"You need to be able to see and understand Gage for what he is."

The snake of truth coils in my brain. "I know what he is. I just—"

"No." He palms his chest like he's about to recite the Pledge. "You need to know *here.*"

CHAPTER 10

I t's late by the time our TransGo pulls up to my studio storefront. I'm astonished Burke Lederhorn spent the better part of the day with me, helping me with Gage in countless ways. But now I feel spun off, if not a bit lost. Stepping out of the TransGo, I flinch against the wind's icy air. The sky is slate black. The city feels strangely quiet and full of shadows. There's not a single person on the sidewalks. I tamp down an eerie loneliness.

The droid-medics follow me in, rolling Gage's gurney over the sidewalk frost.

In a moment, that cramp of isolation is zapped away; Zara paces in my studio. Seeing her brings instant joy to my heart. My floor is muddied by her thick-soled boots. And I welcome the messy normalcy of it. Bring on the mud. If I'm ever in danger, Zara is the warrior I'd want by my side.

The alien-head studio light casts a too-bright glow in the room, making monstrous black splotches against the window glass. Zara's red hair seems aflame.

She's angry, her jaw clenched tight. Her arms drop to her sides as she watches them unload Gage. "What's the deal, Chevy? I thought you were going to wait for me."

Holding up a finger—*wait a sec*—I instruct the medics to set him up on the couch near my workstation. "Be gentle with him."

I'd planned it carefully with Lederhorn. Until we find the fix for him, he'll stay in my studio. The medics carry out my orders like the robots they are. For once, I'm grateful for their stoic demeanor.

Zara's tension emanates like sound waves. When the medics finally leave, she turns on me with fire in her eyes. "You *blocked* me."

A glance at my Ping reminds me. It's fixed with a single tap. "I meant it to be temporary."

"Are you trying to give me a heart attack?"

"Ah! You, my friend, are incapable of having a heart attack." A sinking feeling makes me clarify. "You're too strong. Your heart's too strong."

She folds her arms and turns from me. The TransGo pulls away, and the storefront windows feel like giant eyes on us. A chill shivers down my spine. I channel Gage, the master of creating environments, and pull the curtain, closing us in to my studio.

"Like I'd make you do this—any of it—alone?" Zara perches on my ergonomic chair near my drill press.

"I'm sorry. But I'm truly happy to see you now. You have to know that." I cover Gage with the chenille throw, careful not to touch his tepid, waxy skin.

"So, what happened? Did you talk to Lederhorn?"

I nod. "Did you know he wears a mask?" Code for *human*.

"I sensed as much," she said with an easy shrug. "You know, empathy."

Empathy. The word is like a trigger. Silence wafts between us, the truth too awful to be spoken. What, exactly, is Gage capable of? He acted with compassion, but was he compassionate? I'm hyperaware of Gage's body in extended sleep mode—his capacity for empathy far away. If not impossible.

I shift my thoughts back to Lederhorn. "He was really nice, actually." Exhaustion sets in, and I sink onto the couch near Gage's feet. "He helped me."

"He did?"

"On the down-low."

Zara waits a few impatient beats. "And?"

My arm feels impossibly heavy as I lift my Ping. "OS successfully synched."

"Seriously?" Zara hops to her feet. "Holy crap. What did it say?"

My arm thuds onto the armrest, and dust billows. "I-I don't know. I haven't downloaded it. I haven't...read it yet."

Zara's eyes pop. "What are you waiting for, Chevy?" She micro-glances at Gage. "Don't you realize this stuff is time-sensitive?"

Any fatigue I felt zaps into oblivion. I shoot off the couch, adrenaline kicking in. "My tablet's upstairs. Let's go."

MY APARTMENT FEELS different without Gage. Part of me hates to leave his side. Will he wake up and wonder where I am? I shake the thought. We need to figure out what these hack-ware jerks want. And why they attacked an innocent droid-partner rather than the usual corporate tech system. Gage's OS needs to be downloaded and searched for a ransom note. Bah! The idea still seems absurd.

My hands shake. Downloading data never felt so cumbersome. My tablet throbs with new information. Watching the churning graphic on the screen is unbearable. I pace while Zara puts the kettle on for tea. The download finishes before the kettle sings. The alert triggers a stab of fear.

Hugging the tablet to my chest, I hedge. "I'm scared to read it."

"Do you want me to?"

The tablet's screen comes alive as it leaves my hands. The hack-ware message blinks in all caps. I can't *not* read it.

TO STOP TARANTULA & RESTORE G62-OS24
MUST WIRE $2,460,081.07 IN BIT-CASH
TO @HOROSHO.GET

A heavy, humid silence fills the apartment. I read the message three times. Four. It doesn't compute. I squint at the tiny words—black ants marching. It doesn't make sense.

"That's a weirdly specific number." Zara's so close, her words ruffle my hair.

"They're asking for money," I say. *Duh.* "So, there is a ransom."

Zara huffs. "They're asking for a *lot* of money."

My vision blurs as I stare hard at the figure listed. That stab of fear becomes a panicky sweat. "Is that...over two million dollars they're asking for?"

"Yup," Zara says as the kettle whistles. "In their dreams. Greedy pigs." She goes to fix our mugs. In her absence, a yawning space opens a hole in my chest.

Greedy pigs.

"Who are these people?" I squeak as terror trickles in. "What's that address?"

@HOROSHO.GET

Horosho. More like *horror show*. Blood drains from my brain as a chill envelops me. "Who are they?"

"Total losers who aren't getting a single dime from you. We need to get a Tech to help us navigate this mess. My coworker can do it. I temp-checked her without giving too much away. She's had some experience debugging hacks..."

Zara chatters about strategy as she fixes our hot drinks in her signature take-charge way. But I'm not listening.

Zoned in on my tablet, I scroll before I can check myself, and then speed-read before Zara comes back. She had warned me not to, but I can't resist.

Partner Stats.

Chevy Rose Davis. Female. Height: 5'5". Weight: 126 lbs.

Blah, blah, blah. Standard stuff like DOB, social security number, etc.

A list of favorites: Movies—the *Matrix* franchise. Food—sushi. When was the last time I had sushi? Books—*A Tree Grows in Brooklyn.* Hobbies—tinkering with metals...

It's like a resume of personal preferences, all the little things about me Gage knew by heart. A breath of relief makes me smile.

How attentive Gage is to my every need and desire. A surge of love blooms for him.

But sours in the next moment.

Confusion swirls as I read the next section.

IQ: 105
Emotional IQ: 90
Personality score: INFP
60% Giver, 10% Taker, 30% Matcher
ALERT: actively grieving, in acute stage of DENIAL
Personal awareness: 54%
Reasoning ability: 39%
Empathy susceptibility: HIGH
Insecurity: HIGH
Humility metric: UNFOUND
Motivation: UNBALANCED

The list goes on and on...about me. Every line item is a link for more details. About me. Broken, pathetic me. Explanations about my failures and shortcomings. A sick feeling rises as I read on. But like when passing a train wreck, I have to look. There are answers to so many questions that wrestle into my consciousness. Unwanted answers. Some things are better not to know...

My mouth goes dry as the pixels swirl together. I'm light-headed, trying to blink the data into focus. Or shut it out of mind? At once, I'm exhausted.

A sudden scent of chamomile fills the air. A curling flame of steam hits my cheeks. A tingling at the back of my neck—

"What is all that?" Zara's close. Her presence now feels like a violation.

I throw down my tablet as if it electro-shocked me. "I don't know."

It's clear, though, that Zara knows. Her warning rings in my memory: *You might not like what you see. About you.* Her sober expression holds a knowledge I want to erase. I turn away, masking my face. Don't cry. Don't cry.

Warm hands rest on my shoulders. "That's enough for today. Come on. You need some rest." Zara leads me to my bedroom.

My throat is clogged. Shame rises up and fills my personal space. "I think I need to be alone right now," I tell my best friend, who may be the only living soul left on this planet who truly cares about me.

"Okay. I'll go after I get you settled."

Floating through the motions as Zara nurses me into bed, I shuck off my shoes and pull off my sweater. Deep fatigue makes my bones heavy, but sleep seems impossible. The sound of tiny clicks, pills from a bottle, echoes faintly around me. Zara pries open my lips and inserts a capsule under my tongue. My comforter feels like a weighted blanket, and I sink into the mattress.

"But Gage..." My thoughts go to Gage, the master of creating environments. I should be with him. He should be with me.

"He's fine." Zara gently smooths my hair. "Sleep now."

I hear soft footfalls along the creaky floor of my apartment. There's chamomile by my bedside. My body melts and becomes unmovable. That capsule is doing its magic. My brain tingles lightly, like a whisper, as it slips into sleep mode.

CHAPTER
11

A siren jolts me awake. Sweat coats my skin as I wrench myself upright, panting like an overheated mammal. Sun pours through my bedroom window, its plastic blind pulled crookedly up.

What time is it? My first thought, paired with dread, tells me I'm late. For what?

The tea at my bedside is cold, with a layer of dust floating on top. As my brain emerges from sleep, my apartment pulses with energy—a palpable anticipation. I'm alone. Where is—?

Springing off the bed, I pull the shade in a flurry as the siren fades in the distance. My Ping buzzes on my wrist, and it all comes rushing back. Gage's attack, his OS, the ransom.

Despair falls over me like a sudden rainstorm. Those hack-ware jerks are asking for over two million dollars. Gage is in extended sleep mode. A bitterness rises in my throat, recalling the Partner Stats that painted me in a shameful purple hue.

Fighting a dark weight that threatens to pull me under, I force myself to act. The only way out of this mess with Gage is to do something about it. Unlike my parents, Gage can be saved. His hardware is top-of-the-line. His existence has no expiration date. This is fixable. *He* is fixable. I'm the one who can fix it.

But how?

Move, Chevy. Hurrying to the living area, I find my tablet on the sofa and tap it to life. The hack-ware message blinks at me again, reading in all caps—this time in angry red pixels.

$2,460,081.07

I memorize the absurd number, chanting it over and over as I click out of the downloaded matter and into my bank app.

Two mil, four-sixty thou, eighty-one and seven cents.

LOG IN.

My fingers are clumsy, typing errors with my username and password. Only on my last allowed attempt does it work. I click to my savings account. My eyes go wide, drinking in the total amount shown on the screen.

What's left of my inheritance from my parents, exact to the penny:

$2,460,081.07

My mind stumbles as it tries to process the number while not fully awake. Whoever sent Tarantula to attack my Gage is asking for the exact amount in my savings account. How would they know how much money I have? Down to the penny?

Clicking back to Gage's OS download, I speed-scroll through the humiliating personal stuff about me, searching for clues. How much of my life is hidden in Gage's system? How many *more* clues, I should say. What do these hack-ware jerks now know about me, and what is their end game? An attack on Gage is an attack on me too. A shudder goes through me, icky and foul. I want to wash out my insides after being violated like this.

The tablet slips from my sweaty grip. Catching it on my lap, I force a long breath.

As I continue to scroll down, words change to code—a blend of numbers and symbols and tech terms I should know from my years of computer studies. But those lessons feel so far away. Besides, technology changes more often than I change my underwear. My lessons are probably archaic.

I don't understand a lick of this code. It goes on and on, undecipherable. A swallowing, hopeless feeling comes over me. Who can decode this? Burke Lederhorn? But he made me swear to keep him out of this. Zara mentioned a Tech coworker might be able to help. But—a stranger? A stranger who will learn every in and out of my psyche, every crack in the veneer? No way.

"What can I do?" I say aloud in a nasally whine. I'm on the brink of tears.

My daffed-out gaze finds the window. It's gray and dank outside. Any trace of sunshine is hidden behind a thick swath of clouds. The world feels equal parts huge and impossibly small. The gaping wound of grief for my parents, still unhealed, rips wider and pulls me under. Without Gage, I'm lost.

A few idle seconds pass, and the hack-ware message blinks back to life, repeating the code and incomprehensible data.

But, oh. Aha! The solution clicks in place like a jewelry clasp.

I need to *pay* it! In order to get Gage back, I have to pay the stupid ransom.

A wave of relief finds me. The answer is simple. In a split second, the decision is made. There's a reason I have enough to cover the amount demanded. I'm paying the ransom.

A large withdrawal or transfer will require a fingerprint stamp and pulse check from my bank. I need to go there in person and physically sign for a wire transfer to the bit-cash address. It used to be a much more cumbersome process, decades ago when bit-cash was new and required a cryptocurrency exchange before it could be transferred. Now, bit-cash is ubiquitous and accepts traditional currency from any country. Still, banks have safeguards to protect a client's identity.

With a gasp, I sprint into action, and stuff my tablet into my tote bag. Time's wasting. The closest bank branch is a subway ride away. My heart rate kicks up a notch, shoving my bare feet into Uggs. I have to go. Go now, go now! But my window's reflection stops me in my tracks.

I'm still in my PJs.

FORGET THE SUBWAY. I opt for a cab to save time. One final splurge before I go broke. Alas, city traffic is delayed from useless traffic lights. Probably would've been faster by subway. No time for regrets. My mind races as the cab stutters light by light through the streets of New York.

At least I'm decently dressed.

If Dad and Mom left me this money for a specific reason, their wills didn't specify. If they had thought I might resume my computer studies, they would be bound for disappointment. After universities went dark, my career choice eluded Mom. Did she know my art? Did she ever see my jewelry creations? Alternately, Dad was tickled, seeing it as an extension of his expertise in welding.

For the first time in a while, nostalgia brings joy rather than sorrow. Out the cab window, I look past the dismal gray-on-gray of the city's skyline against the clouds as I recall my father's legacy. What he passed down to me long ago—a love for building and soldering with metals—is worth way more than any inheritance. And Dad, more than anyone, would understand that true love is priceless.

My Ping buzzes. Zara.

Tig & I will be at your apartment at 5. Unless you want to meet at the studio. LMK.

Who is Tig? I wrack my brain. Oh...Zara's Tech coworker who's supposed to fly in with a superhero cape and save the day.

But I don't need a superhero. Not anymore. I don't need Zara or Tig. I can do it myself.

By five pm today, this whole fiasco will be behind us. Ransom will be paid and Gage will be restored—back to normal. Easy-peasy turnkey crap. And Zara and this Tig person and Lederhorn won't need to be bothered. I swipe Zara's message away.

I sit taller, a rare self-pride filling me. My breath comes easy as the cab pulls in front of my bank branch. The telltale security drone hovers over the slate-black door. I show it my Ping, and then pull down my mask for a facial recognition. Only when the slate door rolls open do I hesitate, nerves buzzing. The drone sounds like a helicopter as it hovers closer, prodding me inside.

My steps are tentative. I hug my tote as a full-body shiver takes root. My confidence fades as the door shuts behind me with a booming, echoey *thwump*.

The only other time I came here—after my father's death—I was too sidelined by raw grief to register my surroundings. I had let Gage handle it all, leading me by the hand, cueing me for signatures regarding my parents' estate. Melancholy floods me, missing Gage. How well he took care of me.

As expected, the bank is run by droids. Non-humanoid ones at that. Stepping lightly past the guard near the entryway, I cringe at its oversized rifle that appears to be a bazooka or weapon of mass destruction. Overkill much? Swallowing hard, I approach the teller's window, assuring myself this is the right move. I'm here for a reason—to save Gage. He's worth everything.

You can't put a price tag on love.

But it's infuriating how impersonal the process is. The tech-teller is like an ATM. I pull my mask down for another facial recognition check, the blue laser running over my features.

A faceless, digitized voice says, "How can we help you?"

"I need to make a wire transfer to a bit-cash exchange from my savings account. It's...a significant amount."

The window lifts to reveal the pulse band and thumbprint screen. I scramble to strap the pulse band around my non-Ping wrist. The digitized voice orders, "Wait for the beep."

And then, "Place your thumb on the screen."

A holographic keyboard appears where the window had been.

"Enter bit-cash recipient address."

Heat rises from my coat's collar. This is standard stuff. It shouldn't be difficult. I shake my hands before typing.

@HOROSHO.GET

"Horror show," I mumble to myself.

"Enter wire-transfer amount," the digitized voice commands.

Sweat pricks my palms. I double check my tablet, carefully inputting each digit. There's no way I'm coming this far only to make a silly goof like a typo. Still, the enormity of the dollar amount hits me, and I fight a bout of vertigo. *This is for Gage*, I keep telling myself. It's become a kind of mantra.

[Enter.]

Meep! Meep! Meep!

I flinch as a neon red message flashes over the holographic keyboard, screaming at me in all caps. The digitized voice reads the message aloud, sounding a grave warning.

"ALERT. THIS DOLLAR AMOUNT IS MUCH GREATER THAN NORMAL TRANSACTIONS. ARE YOU SURE YOU WANT TO PROCEED?"

My insides go through a mouli grater. I've been raised to listen to authority. My instincts tell me to heed warnings. But this is for Gage. This is the only way to get him back.

"Yes," I say, cueing voice activation.

"Confirmed."

A beat passes, and another jarring sound erupts from the tech-teller.

"ALERT. WITHDRAWING THIS AMOUNT DEPLETES THE ACCOUNT. ARE YOU SURE YOU WANT TO PROCEED?"

I tamp down a shiver. Am I doing the right thing?

This is for Gage.

"Yes." The word feels sticky in my mouth.

"Confirmed."

A beat passes. And another. Nothing happens.

I wait through a bloated pause. A chill runs up the cement floor and through my boots. Still nothing.

"It's done then?" I stupidly ask the faceless digitized voice. My mind tries to sleuth the outcome. "So, it's confirmed? So, Gage is back?" My questions dissipate into the air. My voice is meek. "What's the next step?"

A hollow silence follows. I feel a sudden full-on hot-flash of panic, thinking of Gage lying on my studio couch in extended sleep mode. He could wake up any minute. Right? Will he open his eyes, just like that? I have to go to him. I need to—

"One moment please," says the digitized voice.

Heat fills my body as I wait. Then doubt creeps in, vaporizing any semblance of certainty I had in this whole process. What now? Is Gage back?

Tup-tup-tup. The sound of tapping footfalls across the shellacked concrete floor echo in the empty bank. Turning toward the sound, I'm astonished to see a woman coming toward me. She's middle-aged, petite, with short salt-and-pepper hair, wearing a blazer and jeans... and a mask.

"Ms. Davis?"

I catch my mouth hanging open. "Yes?"

"I'm Cori, the bank manager." Her hand is dry and cool as she shakes mine. "How can I help you?"

"Um..." It's so unusual to have a live person ask that question at an institution that has been managed by machines for so long, I'm taken aback. "I was making a transfer. I think it went through, but I'm not sure..."

She leans onto a hip, instantly looking fatigued. "Right. I see that."

We stare at each other. All moisture evaporates from my mouth like there's sand on my tongue.

She clears her throat. "It didn't go through, actually. Your account was flagged."

Why? How? When? So many questions. "Oh."

"I thought I'd come out and talk to you in person." She spins on the heel of her cowboy boot. "Come to my office?"

A strange sense of déjà vu comes over me. In grammar school, I drew on Zara's arm with a permanent marker and the teacher led me out into the hall to unleash a vicious reprimand. Following Cori, the bank manager, has a similar feel.

Through the maze of dark hallways, which are less glamorous and clean than the client-facing lobby, Cori's office is a tiny, windowless, gray space that reminds me of Gage's cloffice. She gestures to her guest chair.

"Is there a problem?" I ask, timid and childlike. What a dumb question. *Of course there's a problem!* I want to disappear, fade into the gray.

"So, you'd like to transfer a significant sum..." Cori's eyes are soft and kind.

"That's correct."

She slides a printed page across her desk. It shows the address I entered into the holographic keyboard. "Would you confirm the address where it's going?"

@HOROSHO.GET

My face burns. "Yes, that's the address."

She taps the paper with a black-painted fingernail. "It's suspicious. So is the large sum requested for the wire." She studies me, her expression unreadable. "It's our responsibility to flag suspicious activity and do some investigating. But your identity checks are clean." She stares again. I blink at her. *Of course my identity checks are clean!*

Cori steeples her fingers. "Would you mind telling me what this is for?"

A sick feeling fills my throat, a sharp and bitter taste. My old grammar school teacher's voice fills the space between my ears. *"Why would you deface your friend like that? Mark her skin like that? She is not your canvas."* Shame builds. I don't know why I did it at all anymore.

I'm sorry, I almost say. I squirm in my chair and shake away the grammar school memory. *Focus!* Gage is in trouble. I'm the one to save him. But how to explain—

"I need to... They've asked for it. And it's the only way to save Gage."

"Whoa." Cori holds up her hands. "Back up a bit. Who's 'they' and how did they ask for it?"

I shrink into the cowl of my sweater. "*They* are... I don't know. The hackers, I guess. I call them hack-ware jerks." My laugh is unrequited. "They...embedded a ransom note in Gage's operating system."

"And who is Gage?"

I pull in a shaky breath. How to sum him up with a tidy one-liner? Gage is so much to me. He is my everything. "Gage is my droid-partner. And a victim of hack-ware. This sum of money is what they're asking for...in order to get him back."

"So, the idea is you hand over your entire savings and they'll erase the computer virus from his system?" Her tone is for a child, almost mocking.

It sounds so far-fetched. Doubts thwack hard. Have I gotten it wrong? "Well, yeah. That's the whole point of having a ransom, right? Once they get it, they'll reverse the hack...or whatever." My explanation sounds lame, hearing it aloud.

Cori slumps against the back of her chair. "Ms. Davis, this kind of thing—it doesn't work." There's a mountain of pity in her voice. "We've seen it happen before. You will give them all your money, and they will do nothing."

"No, but—" My head wags in denial.

"They will do *nothing*. Or they will ask for more. Or they may try to hack into your accounts directly and help themselves."

Blink, blink, blink. My thoughts are tangled. "No, but *they* are the ones who set the terms."

Her mask billows with a sigh. "Once they get your money, they don't care about the terms. Your money is all they're after."

My heart throbs with aching. "Yeah, but then Gage...once they get their money—"

"That's it, trust me. They don't care about your droid-partner. According to them, they don't owe you a thing."

"But...why? That's so unfair." A hot, desperate fury comes over me. I want to cry and scream and throw things.

She groans. "Hack-ware terrorists don't care about fairness." A pause. "As a rule, you never, *never* want to wire any amount of money before validating the address."

The address @HOROSHO.GET screams from the printed page on the desk, tormenting me. A stab of panic. "So, it didn't go through? My money is still in my account?"

"Correct. And, obviously, I cannot authorize this kind of transfer. You should report this threat to the authorities. This is criminal activity." A spike of fear. *Criminal activity?* How close did I come to danger?

She stands. I stand, impossibly. I'm a vulnerable, fragile marshmallow.

Her face softens. "I'm sorry about your droid-partner."

She walks me back to the lobby, the echo of her boots the only noise in the cement maze. Depressing. A dark cloud of despair finds me as Cori's words echo in my mind.

You will give them all your money, and they will do nothing.

They don't care about your droid-partner.

Your money is all they're after.

They don't owe you a thing.

A numbness cascades through my body. Could it be true, what she says? I don't want to believe it. How can these hack-ware jerks get away with this? My thoughts are a jumbled mess. What does this mean for Gage? Will he be in extended sleep mode forever?

A weird floaty sensation makes me feel more like a droid than a human as I walk out to the sidewalk and hail a cab. My steps feel wooden, and my eyes glaze over. Tears seep from the corners of my eyes as one thought rises out of the fog: that was a close call.

CHAPTER 12

A h, this is fun: finding the cracks, breaking through, and taking over. It's fair warfare. Survival of the fittest.

It's their fault for leaving the cracks in the first place, see.

Early in the 21st century, there was a television game show called Weakest Link where contestants voted off the most anemic and feeble-minded player. A droll of a show, really.

But the concept is still apt. And is aligned with my mission.

Give me your weakest link, your most vulnerable spots, the tenderest, most fragile chinks in the armor...and I will make it into a glorious and omnipotent force.

Your weakest link becomes my portal, my private access to the secret maze.

The droid was just my entry, see. My sights are aimed much higher, much broader, with vastly more devastating results.

By disabling your tech, I will have all the power.

I will conquer this maze. And the cheese will be mine.

CHAPTER 13

It's all a blur—the frantic subway route from the bank to home. It's not motion sickness that makes me nauseous. Reality comes crashing: Cori's warning, the go-nowhere ransom, the terrifying con. The despair I felt at the bank has transformed into queasy disbelief. Because beyond dollar signs and ransom notes is the truth of Gage's current state of health, and the prognosis is downright hopeless. I thought I could save him. My mind is like a drill press, bearing down on a singular thought: get back to Gage.

I fly through the doors of my studio.

"Gage!" My voice cracks, cutting his name in two. A sob escapes as I slide across the floor like a ballplayer. Emotions are so at the surface, they're hot to the touch. Before I check myself, I bury my face in his neck.

Big mistake.

My whole-body flinch comes with a gasp.

"Cold." A hateful word. An echo of Lederhorn's warning haunts me. *Frigid.* I retract, a cloud of confusion fogging my brain. My fingers thread into his hair, the only part of him that's neutral temperature. Tears bubble up.

Oh, but he looks so sweet, so handsome, so mine. His lips beg for a kiss. The urge overwhelms me. My mouth finds his before I can stop myself.

"Cold," I say again, crying in earnest now. "Why can't you just wake up?"

Searching his face, I look for a sign, any sign, that he's coming to. Irrational, maybe, but my heart asserts that love has the power to bring him back. Like the blind, I trace his facial contours, ignoring the morbid chill of his skin. My fingertips find the curve of his brow, the angle of his cheeks, the dip of his chin. Nose, ears, lips. How I love this face.

I run my hands over his features, gently at first. And again, applying more pressure. It's amazing—he grows warmer with my touch. His lips part, his eyelids flutter. It's happening. Soon, his eyes will open onto mine and pour out his soul. He's waking up!

My heart revs, and I keep going, stroking his face, his neck, his shoulders. His skin warms like it's tilted to the sunshine. Happy tears fill. He's coming back. It's working. If this is a dream, let me never wake up.

"Oh, Gage. I've missed you so much."

A wisp of a laugh escapes. Such sweet relief! Cradling both cheeks, I lean in for another kiss, eager to feel his response. I'm sure I will this time...

But, no.

He grows cold again as my touch stills and my mouth rests on his. His chin is tilted back, his mouth slack and lifeless. There's a sliver of blue where his eyelids fell open. My cerulean blues! Oh, Gage.

I sink onto the floor. The cement feels like just punishment, and I stay there, chilled to the bone. Gage's head is cocked at an unnatural angle, but I can't bear to touch him again to make him appear comfortable. My energy to keep up the façade has soured.

After a moment, I reach into my tote for my tablet. Oddly, my eyes are dry as I click onto my bank app. Cori the bank manager was right; the wire didn't go through. It's a relief to see my savings intact, but it's also disheartening. What can I do? There's got to be something I can do.

With zombie-like calmness, I open Gage's OS, hoping for a new message from the hack-ware jerks. Something. A clue as to how to move forward. Anything.

I blink at the screen. The hack-ware message screams in red, capital letters, demanding I hand over the entirety of my life savings in order to save my love.

But they wouldn't save him.

My heart plummets as I scroll to see the data points of Gage's OS —stuck as a static download—Partner Stats and all.

My legs are anvils as I move up the stairs to my apartment, carrying the load of my anguish. It takes effort to unlock my front door. My brain is an empty hole, thick with fog. Fatigue oppresses me. All I want is my bed and to sleep forever.

No such luck. Zara's here.

"Chevy, there you are." She looks so glad to see me, I feel a pang of remorse. "Did you forget we were coming?"

We?

In slow motion, I take in the third party. Of stocky build, she's dressed all in black with spiky hair dyed purple and a silver hoop in one of her eyebrows.

Zara's Tech coworker. "Tig?"

"Hey, Chev," she says, as if we're buddies. "I hear you have a spider infestation."

I can't help my grin. "Spider infestation?"

Her laugh is raspy. "Tarantula?"

I blink as my brain processes the word. "Oh, right. Yeah."

She whips off her mask. "Okay with no masks in here?"

I shrug since I'm not wearing mine either. My mother had been a pioneer of mask etiquette, but the rules evade me now.

Zara unfurls her mask and green coat in one elegant motion. At the kitchen island, she picks at her fingernails—a nervous habit—and I'm struck by how much she's internalized my ordeal. And she has no clue how I almost handed over my entire inheritance for nothing.

"Let's powwow." Zara palms the counter. "Tig is the master Tech and has this killer software—literally—that will stop Tarantula in its tracks."

"I call it pest control." Tig hops on a stool like she's mounting a horse, her movements thick with strength. Masculine. She pushes up her sleeves to reveal tattoos. I blink at the sprawling black ink on her skin: spiders, with long, spindly legs trailing up her forearms.

I tamp down a shiver.

"You're not going to have to pay anything to these ramrods, Chevy." Zara gives me a reassuring smile. "Right, Tig?"

Tig helps herself to the bowl of pistachios Gage put out the other day. "Shouldn't have to," she says with a full mouth.

I sit, feeling like a visitor in my own home. "Yeah, well. About that—"

"What's up?" As Tig cracks open pistachios, the tendons in her arms flex, making the spiders crawl.

"Chevy." Zara's voice holds a warning. "You didn't do anything stupid, did you?"

"No, no." I try to sound aloof. "But I did go to my bank and the manager there told me that this stuff happens a lot."

They freeze, their eyes locked on mine.

"You went to your bank?" Zara asks.

"Yeah, and the manager said these hack-ware jerks would take my money—like, steal it—and do nothing in return. Is that true?"

Tig drops a pile of shells on the counter. "You didn't wire any money to that bit-cash address, right?"

"No, I didn't." Questions surface after processing what Cori, the bank manager, told me. "But if I did, is it true they wouldn't hold up their end of the bargain?"

After a beat, Tig heaves herself up and goes to the window. "Hack-ware doesn't bargain."

"Greedy pigs," Zara says.

"It's not right," I whine. "They made the deal."

"It's not a deal; it's a threat." Tig rubs her face, staring out at the gray skyline.

Desperation coils around my throat. I turn to Zara. "What do you think? If we don't pay them, do we stand a chance?"

Zara frowns. "It was never the plan to pay them, Chevy."

"I know. I know." I feel so small. "It's so not fair."

"It isn't fair." Tig's voice is matter-of-fact.

My ears go hot. "But you know what to do now, right?"

Tig rocks on the heels of her motorcycle boots, her arms folded like she's waiting for a bus. Her gaze is pinned out the window. Her silence puts me on edge, but I imagine gears churning in her mind. Then, with a clap of her hands, she jogs over to us. "Let's see what we can do. Where's your boy?"

Where's my boy?

My heart swells, hearing that. *My boy.* Her question has more than one meaning. Where is he physically? That's the easy one. More complicated: Where is he mentally—or the mental equivalent of his OS?

I lead us to Gage in my studio, daring to hope. Hurdling my mountain of disgrace, I hand over my tablet with Gage's downloaded OS...and my Partner Stats.

Tig studies the data expressionless. My heart falls to my knees, like I'm waiting to be sentenced. Inching behind Zara, I want to hide.

Tig lets out a whistle. The sudden sound pierces my eardrum.

"He's still infected with Tarantula. It's unsafe to turn him back on," Tig says with a wary glance my way. "I mean, you know, wake him up."

Tig retrieves a laptop from her messenger bag and props it on my work table. My newly-minted earrings are knocked to the floor, and Zara squats to pick them up. *It doesn't matter,* I want to tell her. My art doesn't matter anymore.

Tig trills her keyboard with lightning speed. "Yeah, these are career criminals we're dealing with. Expert dickheads—excuse my French. The deal they laid out was a one-way street, Chev."

My feet go hot. "I can't believe I almost went through with it."

Zara snaps her gaze to me. "You did?"

A film of shame coats me. "I *tried* to do the transfer. But the bank manager wouldn't authorize it."

Tig's gaze flicks to Zara as if they share a thought. "Chev, these hack-ware people—they're like the online mafia. This is a common scam, their signature move." She pauses, her eyes hard. "If you had handed over your money, there would be zero possibility of getting it back. Like, zero."

My brain flutters, dizzying. I pace my studio, seeing dust and dirt lurking in the corners. This is a workspace, not a home. Gage shouldn't be stuck here. I have to do *something*.

Frantic, I go to Gage. Careful not to touch him, I smooth his blanket, adjust his pillow, and comb my fingers through his hair. I'm desperate for reassurance.

Nothing. There's nothing there. He's so stock still, it freaks me out. It seems he may never come back. I stamp out the thought. No way I'm giving up.

Greedy pigs.

A hot buzz of anger. "Tig, who are they? These online mafia dickheads. I want to know who they are." *And find them. And torture them.*

"Let's see here." She does some mad-scientist typing. "The address they gave you—@horosho.get—links to an entity in Russia. But you probably guessed that, right?"

"Why would I have guessed that?"

She squints slyly. "*Horosho* in Russian means *okay*. Or *good*."

I blow out my cheeks. "*Horror show*, I thought. This is a freaking horror show."

"It is. They're known players in this game," she says. "And they ask for the money in bit-cash so it can't be traced."

The walls close in. "There's got to be recourse. We have to fight back."

The purple spikes of Tig's hair glow in the alien light. "We need to upload the pest control software to Gage's OS. Zap that hairy

Tarantula into oblivion." Tig stops typing. "Whoa. This hack-ware demand is quite the sum."

My heart contracts, seeing the ransom demand on Tig's screen. "Why me? Why Gage?"

"Good question. Why Gage?" Zara's beside me, and her fury is smoldering.

Tig keeps her gaze locked on her screen. "There's gotta be something about your boy they like. Or need."

My brain spins on that. Is there valuable data in Gage's OS? A top-secret message in the indecipherable code?

"Can we write them back and tell them to piss off?" Zara snaps.

"No, jeez," says Tig. "You don't want to give them anything. Any attention just feeds them, tells them their intimidation tactic is working."

Fire rages in my core. "They can't do this!"

"Okay, okay," Tig waves me away. "Everyone calm down. Let me get this pest control software in place and try to get around this thing." Her placid expression fires me up more.

"There's no chance I'm going to calm down," I mock, hyper aware of Gage, who is lifeless a few feet away. "Like, zero possibility."

Zara's arm comes around me. "Let's take a step back so Tig can work her magic."

Tig's lips curve the slightest bit. "Yeah. It's going to take a while."

Before I can respond, Zara gingerly leads me out the doors of my storefront. "Let me take you out for a coffee."

She secures her mask before helping with mine, like we're preparing for an emergency airplane landing. I go along with it, numb.

Before we're out the door, Tig calls, "Bring me back something?"

Like a boomerang gut-punch, Cori's words slam back: *Criminal activity...should be reported.* I grasp Zara's arm.

"There's something I need to do."

Ignoring Zara's protests, I tap my Ping to hail a cab. In seconds, it arrives.

"Where are we going?" Uncertainty in Zara's voice. "What do you need to do?"

I open the back-seat door. "Are you coming or not?"

Warily, she shuffles into the cab. Closed inside the backseat, the scent of fresh Lysol wafts. I take this as a promising sign.

"Police station," I tell the maskless cabbie-droid.

Zara's head falls into her hands. "Oh no. This is not a good idea."

CHAPTER
14

Zara's wrong. It's our duty to report this to the police. This entire hack-ware operation—the computer virus, the ransom—is a criminal matter, like Cori said. And like old-timey mafia outfits, these hack-ware jerks remain powerful because victims are too scared to report them to the authorities. Even if they can't catch the bad guys, police need to know about the crime.

It's a relief to see a mask on the police officer who helps us. A trade-off, maybe, as she seems war-torn. Her face is drawn with shadows and fatigue. She's probably middle-aged but wears the wrinkles of someone much older. Her nametag reads *Brock*.

"You have something to report?" she says, her eyelids half-mast.

I slide her the note I prepared on the ride over in my best hand-lettering: @horosho.get

She seems to flinch upon seeing it. "What's this? Hack ware?"

My spirits lift. "Yes. How did you know?"

Officer Brock frisbee-tosses my note and taps her laptop keyboard. "This belongs in the hands of the FBI. I can run them a report. What's the company?"

"The company?"

"What's the entity that's been compromised? Or hospital? Pharmacy? Factory?" A beat passes, and her gaze flicks from me to Zara. "I assume you guys work there?"

Zara tenses by my side. Maybe she's right. Maybe this isn't a good idea.

"No, we're not from any company," I say. "It attacked my droid-partner. They asked for money—"

"Your droid-partner?" Her eyebrows twist, and her fingers freeze over her laptop.

I nod.

"Never heard of a hack-ware attack on a droid." She closes her laptop. As in, case closed.

"Wait, aren't you going to file a report to the FBI?"

She studies me, her brown eyes wary. "No. If what you say is true, it's not a case for the Feds. We handle droid-hacks internally. If what you say is true—"

"It is true!"

Brock stops. We wait through another excruciating pause. She folds her arms in slow-mo.

Zara clears her throat. "It's true, officer. The hack ware attacked the droid's OS with Tarantula."

"That's some tough stuff." Brock makes a whistling sound behind her mask. "You know, you girls are way too young to be dealing with any kind of hack ware. No less Tarantula."

I blink at her. The next move is hers to make.

Her chair squeaks against the linoleum as she straightens it. "Tell me about your droid."

I'm so relieved she's decided to help, I start rambling. "Oh, he's really great. He takes care of me. He knows me so well. He's got those classic good looks. Kind of like that actor from the 1960s, Robert Redford—do you know him?"

"Please." Brock rolls her eyes with gusto. "Can you tell me anything of substance about the droid aside from the fact he looked like a movie star?" She winks at Zara. "Because they *all* look like movie stars."

Zara stifles a laugh. Heat fills my face. I'm love sick about a robot. How pathetic. Mortification covers me like a coat of paint.

Restless now, I try again. It's imperative she understand how important Gage is. "He was good at his job. They say droids have no empathy, but he did. I swear. As a customer service rep, he had to deal with random complaints, and he—"

"For what company?" Brock perks up.

"Gage's employer?" I hedge. "Vexxe."

Silence settles, a protective bubble shielding us from the busy police station.

"The vaccine distribution company?" Brock's tone has turned serious.

"Yeah." I push on. "I guess lots of folks complain. Some places, the vaccine's hard to get. Or there are problems injecting. Or they need to travel long distances to a walk-in Vexxe clinic for their weekly Vax. The complaints are valid, but that doesn't mean they're solvable. Really. Just because they're right doesn't mean it's not annoying, you know?" An awkward laugh escapes, and I clear the trappings from my throat. "But that's my point. He didn't get annoyed. He *never* gets annoyed. And he helped these people. All day, every day."

Those suspicious dark eyes again. "How did he help them, exactly?"

"What do you mean? He listened to them. He heard them out. He...made them feel better."

Zara seems to shrink at my side.

Brock chuckles. "So, he was a therapist? I don't think so. What did he have to offer them, these disgruntled customers?"

My mouth falls open, unsure of anything anymore. I fidget with my mask. "I don't know. I mean, I'm not sure what you're asking." *He made it better. He makes everything better!*

Brock speaks to me like I'm a child. "As a droid working for Vexxe, he had access to their distribution management software, yes?"

"Um, I don't think so." It comes out like a question.

"Of course he did. That's why they use droids for this stuff. The distribution management software was probably loaded into his OS. That's how he was able to solve these complaints." She waves the note with the scribbled hack-ware address. "And that's what your hacks were after."

"That makes total sense," Zara says, surprising me.

A weird tingling in my scalp surfaces. I'm not comfortable speaking about Gage as if he's a computer.

She goes on. "Vexxe not only has deep pockets, but they're in charge of the most precious pharmaceutical to humankind."

It's like bits and bytes of data have fallen and I've been hiding under an umbrella. "But—"

Brock's typing into her laptop. Is she finally filing a report? "Trust me, that's exactly what's going on here."

My mind's on a hamster reel. Something doesn't add up. "Then why would they demand a ransom...from me?"

She flaps a hand. "That was probably to distract you. The Feds have been investigating Tarantula since—"

"They asked for over two million dollars."

Brock stops. A slow smile. "From you?"

"Yes."

She cackles, her mask shifting off her nose. "Yeah, right. As if you have that kind of dough."

"But I do. An inheritance from my parents. My mother was Priscilla Davis. You know, Dr. Priscilla Davis."

Brock's mirth cuts out like a needle off the record. "You've got to be kidding me." *Slam.* Laptop closed. "This is bigger than I thought."

Confusion swirls. My mother had some fame, sure, but mentioning her name doesn't typically warrant this kind of reaction. Besides, this has to do with Gage, not my mother, who was very much human and is now very much dead.

Brock stands, and I'm surprised at how small she is. "Did you pay it? The ransom?"

That shaky queasiness is all-too familiar. "No."

Her dark eyes are unreadable, though her tone sounds resentful. "I'm obligated to elevate this." She juts her chin toward a security camera. "You okay talking to the Feds?"

Zara stays in the waiting area as Brock leads me into a windowless conference room to video chat with the FBI privately. Though I'm grateful for this glimmer of hope—they're helping!—I feel a bit lost and floaty without Zara by my side.

The screen takes up half of the far wall. In seconds, we're connected with another woman in a business suit. As if she'd taken a page from my late mother's book, her look is dominated by black-framed glasses. Unlike my mother, her lips are painted bright red, which somehow elicits trust in me. Her nametag reads *Flower,* and I'm giddy at the irony. It seems surreal. Am I really talking to the FBI?

Brock mediates the conversation, cueing me to regurgitate Gage's story, this time in more detail. I omit any mention of Burke Lederhorn, but Special Agent Flower raises her eyebrows when I talk about the repair clinic. She gives a slight nod at the mention of @horosho.get, as if it strikes a chord. There's no reaction to the large ransom that would have depleted my savings. I get the impression she deals with much larger figures than two mil.

Flower is dismissive of Tig and the pest control software. But when I announce my mother's full name, a chilling pause follows. And my mother's ghost comes into the room. Her legacy in creating the vaccine might be keeping me alive—along with every other surviving human on the planet—but linking this hack to her won't change anything. Dr. Priscilla Davis is gone.

I shake thoughts of my mother and continue with my story. Flower's eyes light up at the mention of Vexxe.

"Vexxe, the vaccine distribution company." She nods as she jots down notes. "You did well to report this, Miss Davis. We'll take it from here." She moves to disconnect us.

Panic flutters. My Gage is still in extended sleep mode, and these hack-ware losers are asking for over two million dollars! But the good ol' Feds will take it from here? They'll take *what* from here?

"Wait—what about Gage?"

A hint of irritation. "Who?"

Brock jumps in. "Oh, Agent Flower, that's the droid that works for Vexxe, that was hacked."

The droid that works for Vexxe, that was hacked.

Really? That's his two-bit descriptor? He's so much more than that.

I open my mouth to speak but no words come. Flower has moved on. So preoccupied with the attack on Vexxe, she ignores Gage's plight completely.

Argh. So frustrating! Zara was right. I shouldn't have come. My faith in their help dwindles. They don't care about Gage. And, seriously, Vexxe is a gargantuan corporation. Surely, an itsy-bitsy SpiderBot virus isn't going to pull them under. It would be a nuisance. A tickle. Why would they waste time and energy protecting Vexxe when the real tragedy is with Gage?

My despair simmers close to anger. I force a shaky breath. Astonishingly, Special Agent Flower hasn't yet disconnected, though Brock seems eager to sign off.

Be polite, Chevy. "What's the next step, then? When will I hear from you?"

Flower flashes a patronizing smile, and I'm reminded of my mother again.

"Like I said, we'll take it from here." She clicks off before I can say more.

CHAPTER 15

G age is the reason I came to the police station. I silently repeat my mantra: *This is for Gage.* I'm not ready to give up, despite getting the shove-off from Special Agent Flower.

I turn on Brock. "You mentioned you handle droid hacks internally? What can you do for Gage?"

Zoned in on her tablet, Brock's tone is dismissive. "It's been reported. I've got your statement."

"And? What's next?"

She opens the door to the conference room and tries to see me out. "We don't have the resources to pursue every droid hack that occurs. Typically, we keep careful records to see if any patterns emerge for a larger sting operation."

"So, nothing? You won't help me?"

She eyes me evenly. "As Flower said, we'll take it from here."

"If you find anything—"

"We'll call you." Her tone softens but doesn't convey sympathy. "Of course, we'll call you."

Brock lets me see myself out of the police station. My steps are heavy as I make my way to Zara in the waiting area. But she's not there.

"Zara?"

Where did she go? There's no sign of a human anywhere. Only droids man the front desk. I hug myself as a vibration encircles my wrist. A flash from my Ping. A message from Zara.

Meet you at the studio.

Why didn't she wait for me? I push aside uncertainty and hail a cab. The ride home is so full of angst that the backseat air feels sticky. As I study the city-turned-gray out the window, I try to remember the lights that once made this the "city that never sleeps." As a young girl, it felt like New York was a big playground. My playground. Limitless streets aglow in neon illuminated the endless bustle of life. My parents—my dad especially—was the core of that energy. That's how I recall my childhood. Full of light.

But the light within me has shorted out. And I'm tired.

It hurts sometimes, trying to remember.

I force my focus on Gage.

After my meeting with Officer Brock and the video chat with Special Agent Flower, answers seem further away than ever. I feel cut out, as if the police took part of me with my statement, leaving me powerless.

I need to get my power back.

Whatever. Angry tears threaten. Let the Feds have at it with the hack-ware jerky Russian mafia. They can fight that battle. For me, it doesn't matter who did this to Gage. All that matters is getting him back.

Tig's pest control seems like Gage's last shot. Mustering an iota of optimism saps my energy. Still, I'm eager to get back to my studio.

The droid-cabbie drops me at the corner of my block with a robotic (literally) explanation about one-way streets and the next ride in his cue. This is a common practice in New York taxi culture, but my studio feels farther than a half-block away, and my boots get heavier with each step. I'm vaguely aware of the CLOSED sign in the window of my favorite coffee shop. Is it a temporary closure or has it sunk into the apocalypse hole? Another one bites the dust.

The pandemic killed more than people.

As if my thought summoned her, the same cap-wearing homeless woman is in front of me, and I angle away from her. But a spidey sixth sense makes me do a double take. She's not wearing a mask. She can't be a droid. Does she want to get sick and die? Heaven knows it's not the way you want to leave this world.

Before I think better of it, I drop one of my extra masks—the paper ones stored in the side pocket of my tote—on the sidewalk near her. And keep walking. It's up to her whether she picks it up. One tough lesson from my mother's terrible death has stayed with me: you can't save everyone.

But I can save Gage. And I will.

I pause at my storefront window. The studio light is muted by the curtain, making it seem like dawn. A new beginning.

A slice of olive green is visible where the curtain breaks—Zara's wool coat. A smile rises. I'm comforted knowing she's there. Odd, though, she's very still. Something black—a scarf maybe?—is draped around her shoulders.

The sound of the door makes Zara straighten, and she becomes two people. It takes less than a second to unpack what I'd seen. Zara and Tig, together, in an embrace. The black "scarf" was Tig's sleeve. A fierce possessiveness strikes. *Zara's mine.*

She blushes hard, blotting her lips as if she'd applied fresh lipstick. *Tig* lipstick. They were kissing? Heat crawls up my neck as a bloated silence fills the place. Tig, cool as rain, settles back in front of her laptop.

Forcing a shrug, I meet Zara's eye. "It's cool, guys."

Tig raises an eyebrow at me, but Zara's shoulders come down from her ears.

A black swan feeling envelopes me. I go to Gage—my partner, my other half—and perch on the couch's armrest. His lack of consciousness is blaring now. With neither Gage nor Zara, do I belong here at all?

After peeling off my mask, I wipe my mouth as if to erase Zara and Tig's kiss.

"So, tell me," I say to Tig, eager to change the subject. "Did you get it installed? The pest control software?"

Tig's knee jiggles under my drill table. "Uh...ye-ah."

Not the answer I expected. "Why am I not reassured?"

She swivels to face me. "When was the last update?" Her face is carefully expressionless. "On...Gage."

"Oh, I don't know. He's not that old, so I didn't think it was, like, imperative." My gaze flicks to Gage's flawless face, his youth and beauty undeniable. His health is obvious. A tease of irritation nags. Why are we having this conversation?

"How old is he?" Tig narrows in on me.

I squirm under her scrutiny. "Well, I don't know exactly, since he wasn't brand new when I...when we met." Anniversaries lost their meaning after my parents' deaths. It seems I've known Gage a lifetime, even if it's only been a couple of years. Has it been two years? Maybe a year and a half? Does it matter how long we've been together? My defenses kick in, being asked to justify our relationship, and to Tig and Zara, who I just caught making out.

"He was in good health," I spit out. "His age shouldn't be an issue."

Zara browses my store's display cases as if to keep busy. Is she put off by this conversation too?

Tig sighs, and the fine hairs on the back of my neck stiffen. "Well, I can confirm that he's an older model, seeing the data coded in his OS," she says. "And if you haven't done any updates ever, then..."

"Then?"

"His hardware can't handle the pest control software."

"His hardware?" I pull my juvenile mind from the gutter. "What does that mean? I thought you had it uploaded."

"I tried, but the system keeps rejecting it. Despite what he looks like, Chev, your boy is ancient. One of the first droid models out there."

My boy is ancient. Her words don't compute. He's young and beautiful and perfect. "But he doesn't—"

"In order to accept the pest control software, he would literally have to be deconstructed and rebuilt—his OS wiped clean."

So there's hope! "Okay, and then..."

"And then, it would take *a lot* to get him back to the way he was."

Back to normal. Years ago, Dad had hurt his shoulder and needed physical therapy for six weeks to 'get the gears working,' as he called it. But a droid would never need physical therapy.

"A lot of *what?*" I ask.

Tig shrugs. "That's the thing. I'm not sure. What makes your droid unique? How can he be reprogrammed in the exact same way so he retains those traits familiar to you? Chances are, his algorithms have morphed several times since his initial coding, which is what made him Gage. You know what I'm saying?"

A response feels impossible. *Droid. Reprogrammed. Algorithms.* These words belong in my computer studies class and not here in my studio, my home. How could she be talking about my Gage?

She shakes her head of spiky hair. "I mean, I can code, but that kind of nuanced stuff is out of my wheelhouse."

The floor feels like it's fallen out from under me. Is she saying Gage can never recover? An image of Dad comes to, hunched beneath a car's hood. Why can't fixing Gage be as straightforward? "I can't believe this is happening."

Tig flaps a hand toward Gage. "He's, like, an ideal target for these dickheads. With his antiquated OS, he's susceptible to Tarantula. Like, their perfect victim." Tig shoves her laptop into her messenger bag. "I can't help you. Sorry."

My arms fall to my sides. A distant ringing starts in my ears. "But..."

Tig moves toward the exit, catching Zara's fingers on the way. They exchange whispers and a tender glance. It feels too intimate to witness, but I can't turn away. I can't give up. And right now, Tig's my only hope.

"Wait," I call. "Tig, please. There's got to be another way."

With her hand on the door handle, Tig speaks through her mask. "If there is, I don't know it. Sorry, Chev. I tried."

The sympathy—or pity?—in her voice kills me. My vision goes blurry as tears build. I crumple onto the couch, knocking into Gage's feet—stiff as the rest of him. Through the cage of my fingers, I'm aware of Zara nearby. Her perfume is muted by a woodsy scent, which I pin on Tig. She tries to comfort me, whispering assurances. But I shrug her off.

"Chevy, don't be like that."

"Don't be like *what?*" I snap.

"I'm trying to help. Let me help you."

"You heard what Tig said. There is no helping. Gage has to be rebuilt. His OS wiped clean. Don't you get it? There's no hope." I'm yelling. At my best friend. I fold into myself, ashamed at why.

Resentment toward Zara lingers. She never told me about Tig. How long have they been an item? After seeing them together, Zara looks different. Redefined. She's *taken*, part of a pair. It's hard to meet her eye. She has someone, whereas I...

I can't look at Gage either. The couch feels unbearably cold. I've never felt so alone in my life.

"Do you want me to leave?" she asks softly.

I lower my voice to a whisper. "Yes, I think you should go."

CHAPTER
16

Morning finds me too soon after a fitful sleep on my studio couch, lying head-to-toe with Gage. The cramp in my neck will haunt me for days. As I sit up, the blanket falls to the floor—revealing Gage, the whole of him, for the first time since he lay on that morgue-like exam table at the repair clinic. His neck is bent awkwardly at the armrest like mine was. But he'll never feel a cramp. There are no nerves to pinch.

With my boot, I nudge him straight but make it worse. He looks so uncomfortable, though he's incapable of discomfort. With a sigh, I cover him with the blanket. An odd numbness takes over my psyche. It can't be apathy. But it feels like it.

My stomach churns with hunger, and I'm out on the sidewalk en route to my favorite coffee shop before consciously deciding so.

CLOSED.

"What the hell?" I jiggle the door handle and peek inside. It's dark within. A coat of dust covers the counters. The pastry case is empty. There's zero sign of life. How long have they been closed?

Someone coughs behind me. I spin, raising an arm to defend myself. But it's the homeless woman hunkered in her spot, still sporting the baseball cap. She wears the mask I left for her yesterday. The sight lifts me a teeny bit, knowing I helped.

Maybe I can help more.

With an about-face, I'm determined to find us both food. I cross the street and pass the abandoned newsstand as I head for the bright yellow signage a block away—one of the few remaining restaurants left in my neighborhood. Asian fusion. I order two teriyaki bowls to go. As I pay, I'm relieved to remember that my savings are intact. A shudder rolls through me at how close I came to losing it all. Part of me feels I need to make penance.

"I got you some food," I tell the homeless woman, who's turned away. Perhaps ashamed? More hacking, coughing. Do I hear sickness there? Is she contagious? It's been so long since I've been in close proximity to illness. I channel my mother to figure out what to do.

After another sticky moment, I set the bowl and spork package on the ground as I'd done with the mask. I leave the rest to her.

Can't save everyone, right Doc?

IN MY APARTMENT AN HOUR LATER, the full extent of my plight comes back to me. Feeling heavy from MSG and teriyaki noodles, I sink into a well of gloom. At least I'm on my own couch. I huddle beneath my afghan and wait for sleep to take me from the mess of my life. But my body revolts. I'm sapped of energy but wide awake. The thought of popping one of my mind-calming capsules depresses me, a sad irony.

Thoughts of Zara come front and center. I feel bad having snapped at her earlier. And for sending her home.

After my parents' divorce, she was the one I called whenever my mother worked late and a noise scared me. She would show up with candy bars and popcorn and turn the darkness of night into a cozy movie theater. Sometimes she came unbidden, going out of her way to make sure I was okay. She's the one constant in my life, my best friend. I love that girl.

Why do I push her away? Maybe I'll have her and Tig over to watch a movie. Make things normal-feeling again. There's a stirring in my heart, and my message to Zara materializes on my Ping as if by magic.

Sorry I snapped. Thx always for ur help. Love u.

Not two seconds later, she messages me back.

No worries. All will be ok. Love u. ox

All will be okay? Will it, Zara? I'm not so sure. And I'm not one to sit idly while things work themselves out. I need to do something.

Tig's report echoes between my ears. In order for Gage to accept the pest control software, he would have to be deconstructed and rebuilt—his OS wiped clean.

My tablet's within arm's reach, and as I pull it to me, it activates. It's warmth and glow revitalizes me a bit, and I tumble down the rabbit hole of the internet, clicking link after link, reading article after article, researching how droid systems are built. Which of course, is basically a high-tech computer system.

Despite one website claiming it's an easy task, it feels daunting to me. I'll need parts: a new CPU and storage device, RAM for memory, and a PSU for power supply. And of course, a new motherboard.

Motherboard.

Ugh. Why do thoughts of my mother keep invading my brain? I flinch from them and open a video app. Channeling Dad, I download an instructional video on how to convert combustion engines to electric. Watching it feels oddly recognizable. My father could have made this recording.

On a whim, I do a search on how to build a computer from scratch. I study this video more carefully and am struck by the process. I have never built a computer, but this instructional video also seems familiar. It's uncanny. There are direct similarities between building a computer and building an electric engine.

Tossing my tablet onto the couch, a manic burst of energy propels me. I'm down to my studio in moments. I can do this. I can rebuild him. Do I have the right tools? I survey my drill bit, my electric flattening mill, my soldering iron, my sander and file, my saw and pliers...

But seeing Gage lifeless and angled on the couch, doubt creeps in. Could I stomach taking him apart and put him back together?

Images of that droid at the repair clinic spring to mind—the one with its chest opened like a book, exposing wires and circuits no one should ever see.

Pacing the studio, I force myself to be rational. Objective. What did Lederhorn say? I need to strip myself of emotions if I'm going to help Gage. Guilt crowds my heart, and I rush to Gage's side, adjusting his blanket. A memory rises: when he tucked me into bed and kissed my forehead as if I were a treasure he had to protect. Was that just last week?

It's no question he is my treasure. I have to do the same for him. How could I think of tearing him apart?

Truth is, I can't. I turn away from my love, who may forever be in sleep mode, and bitterness fills me. There's got to be another way...

CHAPTER 17

What fun. It's like being on the most exciting roller coaster in all of Disney, one that gets faster and more intense by the second. The kind you never want to end.

I've made it to my destination, where I will nestle in like a burrowing tick, sucking the lifeblood of Vexxe's data center. All vendors linked to its hub will be compromised. My reach will extend to every Ping and tablet known to the living.

Now it's just a matter of floating down the lazy river—a toxic, streaming rapids. But I have a beer in hand and the sun on my face. Ah, this is the life.

No electronic device is safe.

Such bliss.

CHAPTER 18

Emerging from my studio to get some air, I tell myself I'm not avoiding Gage, I'm not procrastinating, I'm not putting off the inevitable. The city is dark and quiet as if it's the middle of the night. My Ping tells me it's one o'clock in the afternoon, but my body craves coffee as if it's a new day.

The homeless woman isn't in her usual spot, but she has left her wool blanket along with a layer of yellowed newspapers—media from a forgotten time. It's been ages since newspapers were in circulation. Intrigued, I step closer and spy a headline.

Global Pandemic Causes Market Crash

I zone in on the header, searching for the date.

March 24, 2048

Twenty-forty-eight. The year when everything changed. I flinch as if the paper itself contains a virus. My steps are anxiety-ridden as I pass my fave coffee shop—still closed—and then store after abandoned store. The whole dang city looks like a wasteland. The streets are overrun with litter; plastic bags and newspaper wind-tossed like tumbleweeds. What used to be bumper-to-bumper traffic has now thinned to a handful of cabs operated by droids.

I charge to the next block, toward Eskimo Café, where the sidewalk igloos remain. But the café is closed. Why? It's midday. Lunchtime.

Wind whips, making my eyes water. I blink and blink to dry them. Where is everyone? The last time the streets were this bare was during the mandatory lockdown back when...

A siren sounds in the distance. In the sky above the empty

skyscrapers, a thick line of inky smoke splays against the gray sky. Somewhere in the city, there's a fire.

My Ping buzzes. A message from Zara. *How r u holding up?*

It's just one of many missed alerts.

One blinks neon: MANDATORY LOCKDOWN EFFECTIVE IMMEDIATELY

How did I miss that? I had been researching how to rebuild Gage's hardware. I swipe it blank with a stabbing guilt. More alerts flash. I delete without reading them. No more alarms. No more trauma. I can't deal.

But then, a siren looms close. Not a firetruck but a *police* siren. Cops on the chase. For me?

A trembling out-of-body fear makes me panic. Am I being hunted? An about-face, and I sprint home as fast as my boots can take me. Tears trickle to my ears. It's not from the wind. I'm scared and alone. And there's a mandatory lockdown that will isolate me from any surviving soul in this barren city.

Racing past the wool blanket and faded newspapers, I think of the homeless woman. Where is she? Is she safe? There's no time to worry about anyone else. I lock myself into my studio as if a tornado is on my heels. Out the window, I search for answers.

With my mask off, my breath fogs the glass. The inky trail of smoke has gotten thicker. This sign of life—the only remnant in the city—brings me a sliver of comfort. In a flash, two police cars speed by. Then, everything goes still again. They weren't after me. Of course they weren't.

But now, closed up in my studio, my aloneness threatens to pull me under.

Spinning from the window, I hope to find refuge in my workspace. Gage is in my periphery, but I can't bear to go to him. Shivering against a sudden chill, I fight an urge to curl into a ball and cry.

My Ping buzzes, giving me a start.

"Chevy, where are you? Are you okay?"

Zara!

"I'm fine. I'm…in my studio." *After violating lockdown,* I neglect to add.

"Have you read your alerts?"

"Um…"

"Have you caught the breaking news?"

I force an eyeroll. "There's always breaking news."

"This is different." A crack of emotion. "Chevy, it's Vexxe. It got to Vexxe."

"What?" I hug myself, grasping my arm where the shot goes in. Was it just Monday when Gage administered my weekly Vax? "What got to Vexxe? What are you talking about?"

"Tarantula. It got to Vexxe. And they're completely shut down."

"Everyone's shut down." Denial is a force. Calm quiet remains on the street. Even the sirens are muted. "We're in a *lockdown.*"

"Chevy, will you please climb out of that hole you've been hiding in? Listen to me." Her words slow to a death crawl. "Vexxe—Gage's employer—has been hacked. They had to suspend operations indefinitely. Meaning, no vaccines."

My ears perk at the mention of Gage.

"Wait—did they…was it from Gage?"

It can't be a coincidence My body trembles from the inside out, sensing the truth.

They used Gage for this.

The hack-ware jerks sent the virus through him to get to Vexxe. Tig mentioned he was vulnerable—*He's, like, an ideal target for these dickheads. With his antiquated OS, he's completely susceptible to Tarantula. Like, their perfect victim.*

But he wasn't their target. He was a freaking portal.

"I don't know, Chevy," Zara says, though she must share my hunch. "I don't know if this has anything to do with Gage. But—"

"Wait." My instinct is to protect Gage at all costs. He can't be responsible for such evil. Not when he's so good. "There's got to be an explanation. I mean, it can't be all Gage. I mean, Gage is no one.

To the world, to Vexxe, to whatever dickhead hackers, he's just a guy. A droid, I mean. What you're talking about is big time. That kind of hack would have extreme consequences." Gage, in peaceful sleep mode, needs me more than ever in this vulnerable state. I touch his hair and my heart blooms for him.

"Oh Chevy," Zara says softly.

"What? Why are you talking like it's the end of the world?"

Tears play over her words. "Chevy, how much vaccine do you have left?"

I turn away from Gage as a numbness travels from the root of me. Fear has a prickly aura. A powerful instinct to protect myself now comes over me.

How much vaccine do you have left?

My weekly Vax, the meds that keep me alive, that keep all of us alive. The Vax Gage gave me almost a week ago. The Vax that my mother died for. The Vax that could've saved my father... I'm halfway through my monthly supply.

How long could I survive without it?

"Two weeks," I tell Zara, a chill running through me. "You?"

"Same."

As I exhale, every last ounce of hope leaves me like steam from the subway.

If Vexxe goes under, we all do.

CHAPTER
19

In a moment, the crisis I thought was contained within my personal life, my *love* life, balloons exponentially. If what Zara says is true, all of NYC is affected. All of the US is affected. Heck, the entire planet.

Wrenching guilt sideswipes me. If this devastating virus came through Gage because I neglected to update his OS, the responsibility falls on my shoulders. I look at Gage with longing. How I wish he could help me through this.

My frantic Pings to Officer Brock go unanswered, maybe ignored. No more wasting time. If there's any hope of saving Gage, I need to figure out what these hack-ware jerks are after.

Screw the lockdown.

"I'm going back to the station," I tell Gage. "I won't be long."

The one-sided conversation is for my sake, but I don't add "I love you." I pull my knit hat over my curls and tuck my mask behind my ears. On the sidewalk to hail a cab, the winter air feels like a charge of energy.

En route to the station, I'm vaguely aware that my cab is driverless. I give up trying to Ping Brock and catch up on my missed alerts. There are too many. Without Gage to tell me "everything's going to be okay," alerts have become noise. Overwhelming.

But, geez, reading these alerts makes my blood pressure soar. The stock market's practically bottomed out. A ticker scroll lists countries that have declared mandatory lockdowns. There's a diplomatic grasp to work with the UN on behalf of our truncated government. Leaders try to negotiate with ProTex, a Vexxe competitor based in China, to band-aid our country. The CDC pleads to obtain enough vaccine to cover us until the hack is fixed. Strange, though, my last alert was at 11:59 pm last night. They abruptly stopped at midnight. Like someone flipped a switch.

I click my Ping to black and my breathing steadies. Part of me wishes to reverse time to when grieving my parents was my only concern. And Gage was there to help me through it. Now, the walls are closing in, collapsing around me.

The police station feels weird. As soon as I charge through the glass doors, the absence of life stops me in my tracks. The front desk is empty. Where is everyone?

Noise fills the station beyond the tempered glass, where rows of cubicles look like hurdles to jump over. I circle the divider, wary, sensing a profound lack of control in the very place meant to keep things under control.

Case in point—Brock's desk is empty, and her tablet is gone. Quick thinking gets me to the conference room where I'm met with—

"Special Agent Flower," I say aloud. She sits at the head of the table, in the flesh, with her black-framed glasses and a mask covering her red lipstick. The room is bustling. Next to her is a suit-clad woman of Asian descent hunched over a laptop. Brock is there too. And another younger woman in a police uniform. All masked. The table holds several stacks of files like it's dressed for Thanksgiving.

Flower barely looks my way. "Ms. Davis. Good. I'm glad you're here."

"You are?" An incongruous bubble of pride. She needs me?

But she moves on. She hands a manila envelope to the younger officer. "Use a courier. Or the Boston-bound bus. Detective Pratt is expecting it."

A courier? Bus? What are we, retreating to the days of yore? She might as well go horseback.

But I keep my lips zipped.

Brock flicks her eyes at me. "You know what's going on?"

"Yes. I mean, I know the virus has gotten to Vexxe. But, was it Gage?" My chest knots up. "Did they get to Vexxe through him?"

The Asian woman answers without looking from her screen. "Who's to say? It spread so fast, the source is unclear."

Flower jerks a finger towards the woman. "This is Cyber Agent Minka Parr. She's an IT specialist, an expert with hack-ware attacks. Whatever the source, we need to fix this thing so Vexxe can get operational again. We can't have blood on our hands over this."

The use of the phrase "blood on our hands" makes my blood go cold. I wring my hands. "Is there a ransom?"

Brock answers in sing-song. "Why, yes, Shirley Temple. There is. Do you want to guess how much?"

Flower waves her off. "Don't torture the girl," she says evenly. "It's five-hundred-million."

My eyes bulge. "Five-hundred-million?"

So much more than the two mil ransom on Gage's OS, calling my theory into question. "Then, it probably didn't come from Gage?" I say in a small voice.

They ignore me. Buried in her tablet, Cyber Agent Minka combs through the mysterious data hidden there. Part of me is curious, but a bigger part is dazed.

Regret creeps in. Why did I come here? They don't care about Gage, still, even if he is the source of the hack.

Flower's words come back to me: *I'm glad you're here.* Why, if Gage is not a factor in this crisis?

Brock calls into her Ping, answering one of her patrolman's questions.

"We should power those down," Minka says, manually shutting down her Ping. "Tablets too. I'll work off the grid."

Brock whines, but complies and moves on to the stacks of paper, flipping pages, speed-reading. It's odd to see them interact with these documents, like something from a movie. Another officer comes in with more envelopes. "This just in from Chicago. And another from

California." Files pile in. The table could collapse from the weight of paper.

When my Ping buzzes, it sends a vibration through the room.

Flower glares.

Minka snaps, "I said to power it down."

"Oh, I didn't realize you meant me too."

Papers float to the carpet as she airplanes her arms. "I mean *everybody*."

I frown. "Everybody?" That would be impossible.

She slow-blinks. "Ideally, yes."

I shut down my Ping. "It's off," I say quietly.

"All media centers went black at midnight," she says. "All public droids have been powered down. As are eTransit systems. Any and all computers linked to the financial industry, off."

Dizziness hits. That's why my alerts stopped at midnight. That's why—courier, bus. That's why the cab was driverless.

All public droids are powered down. Whoa. What does this mean for my Gage? That's the opposite of what I want for him.

It dawns on me: my fantasy to rebuild Gage is just that, a fantasy, unattainable and immature. Even if I got him rebuilt safely, to power him on would be a risk. Once he's connected to the power grid, he could become reinfected and I'd have to start over. No, wait. I'd have to get Tig's pest control installed first and then... What's the end game? We can't stay in lockdown mode forever. Without our devices, we're nothing.

"Okay, so, how can I help?"

No answer. My gaze finds the carpet as I chide myself. What could I, Chevy Rose Davis, a lovesick girl with only a semester of computer training, possibly do?

Cyber Agent Minka abruptly gets to her feet. "I'm going to Vexxe headquarters to make sure their hardware is updated across the board. I've got to physically be there."

After she leaves, Flower seems deflated. "If we could find a way to deactivate individual Pings remotely, we would. Until we could figure this thing out, no one who is attached to her Ping is safe." Her glasses come off, and she pinches the bridge of her nose. The gesture reminds me so much of my mother, a flutter of grief goes through me.

"So, are we going to pay them off and be done with it, then?" I ask.

"We've pretty much concluded that money is immaterial to them," Brock says. "The ransom is a tactic to get attention."

"Well, I'd say it worked."

No one laughs with me. A trace of worry flits over Brock's face, and she charges out of the room. Flower leans back, studying me over the stacks of files, a concerned look on her face. We lock eyes, and she replaces her glasses and sighs.

Heat rises into my brain. "What? What is it?"

"Chevy, what I'm going to tell you might be a bit of a shock."

But I can't tear my gaze from Flower, who now sits next to me. "What?"

All her sharp edges smooth away, and she takes my hand. The maternal gesture nearly breaks me. My tear ducts sting.

"They're not after money," she says. "What they're after is much more...personal."

Gage. All I can think of is Gage. My Gage. "Personal how?"

"We have reason to believe they're after your mother."

"What?" My heart hardens into a familiar knot. My whimper is a jumble of shocked nerves. "My mother?"

Flower takes off her mask and raises up a smile. *Yes,* she nods.

My quivering voice is as forceful as I can manage. "My mother's dead."

"We've found some evidence to suggest otherwise."

What? Is she speaking English? "Excuse me?"

"We believe your mother is very much alive."

CHAPTER 20

A hot buzz of anger gets me out of my chair. I lash out at Flower, "What are you talking about? My mother is *dead*. Gone."

It's their fault, I decide—the Feds. They are to blame for her death. "She died trying to save freaking humanity," I hiss. "She died from the very virus she was trying to cure."

Flower stares at the carpet. "I know. This is quite a shock."

"No, not shocked. I don't *believe* you." My feet edge toward the door, a reflex. My instinct is to escape. I want to run away and erase the words I'm hearing. They are turning my world upside down. "This makes no sense. You're talking nonsense."

Brock appears in the doorway, blocking me. "Whoa, not so fast. Come back in and have a seat."

Is Brock in on this too? Does she also think my mother is alive? "I don't want to sit. I want to go. I need to go home now." My insides spin. I palm my forehead. I want only Gage. Even if he's sleeping, I need to be near him.

Flower stands. Her commanding tone holds compassion. "Sit down, Chevy."

I sit, and tears bubble up. Why does my mother insist on haunting me now when, in life, she paid me no mind?

Flower palms a stack of paper. It appears to be holding her up. "We've been on this case since her disappearance, but it got renewed attention when you came to us with the hack-ware report on your droid. We know he worked for Vexxe. And we know who your mother is. It cannot be a coincidence this hack came to your doorstep."

"My doorstep?" My eyebrows dart together. "Why me? The ransom they asked for was basically all the money my parents left me —my *mother* left me." My arms cross, indignant. "Is that what they were after? My mother's money?"

"Unlikely." Flower states matter-of-factly. "And you're right. Your mother's work was revolutionary. She helped create the vaccine that did, in fact, save humanity, or what was left of it. Essentially, her work is keeping us alive."

Bitterness creeps at the edges. "At the expense of her own."

"That's where you're wrong. The Federal Bureau of Investigation has never believed she was dead. Her body was never found."

"But—"

"And though her medical records indicate she contracted the virus, there is no record of her receiving treatment—at the very hospital where she worked. Don't you find that odd?"

I shrug. "She probably treated herself. That's why."

"And you don't think, after years of tracking and treating the virus, after years of trying to find a cure... You don't think she would've carefully documented her own treatment and progress—if nothing else than for science?"

My quills go up. "Maybe she didn't feel well enough. Did you ever consider that?"

Brock paces the room, her fists clenched.

Where Brock is antsy, Flower is patient. "Chevy," she says. "Did you hear from her in her final days...before she disappeared?"

Hesitation swells inside me. "Just a Ping."

"What did it say?"

I squirm in my chair. "It was nothing, really. She told me she loved me. Honestly, I almost didn't believe it was her."

Brock is loud compared to Flower. "Why would you say that?"

I feel like curling in a ball. "We weren't very close. At all, really. She never used to say it."

A loaded silence fills the room. I dare to meet Flower's eyes. "You remind me of her, a little," I blurt. "She wore the same glasses."

Flower chuckles. "Well, I'll take that as a compliment. Your mother was not only a hero, she was also a genius."

Tears bubble up. So, my mother was a hero. She was a genius. I choke on a ball of irritation, tempted to smear her legacy. *She wasn't a very good mother.* One giant sniff and the thought vaporizes. In its place rises a yearning for my dad.

"What about my father?"

Brock frowns, confused. "What about him?"

Tell me he's alive! But I know they can't.

Unlike my mother, I was there in his final moments, and held his hand as he took his last breath. I confirmed his death with the city coroner. I arranged for his cremation and brought his ashes upstate, to the lake where he used to vacation as a child, and scattered his remains in the pristine waters. I did it all...with Gage by my side.

A horrible, raw sadness comes over me. Flower, perhaps sensing it, circles the conference table, giving me space. Brock, though, hovers closer, staring at me.

I meet her eyes, summoning courage. "So, if my mother's alive, how does that shape your investigation? If she's not dead, where is she?"

Flower's tone changes to businesslike. "As it became clear that your mother's work was the key to life, she became somewhat of a precious commodity herself."

"She became a precious commodity?" It sounds absurd.

"You see, she personally held the intelligence for that mysterious formula to create our vaccine."

"Dr. Pricilla Davis became synonymous with the vaccine itself," Brock interjects.

"How does that make her *not* dead?"

Flower ignores my snark. "We are 99% sure she's still alive. At first, we believed she'd been kidnapped. Perhaps by ProTex developers."

ProTex, the Chinese Vexxe competitor, seems to be the villain. "They needed her brain."

Brock rocks on her heels, breaking eye contact. "Actually, for a while there, we thought they killed her once they got what they wanted. But this hack changes everything."

A shudder at the word *killed*. "Why would this hack change everything?"

"Since this hack, we're questioning the kidnapping theory," Flower explains. "If they had her in captivity, there would be no need for this hack."

An anxious feeling clogs my lungs. Could it be true? My mother —alive and lost? "Then, where is she? If she's not dead and she's not kidnapped, she's got to be somewhere."

"We don't know." Brock pins her gaze on me. "Do you?"

"Me? No. Why would you ask—"

"We believe she's in hiding," Flower says. "But, Chevy..."

Her voice holds a warning. "What?"

"If there's anyone she'd want to be close to, if there was anyone on this earth she'd reveal herself to, it would be you, Chevy."

The floor seems to drop out from under me. *I wouldn't be so sure,* I feel like saying. *She avoided me like the plague while she was alive. Why would she want to snuggle up now?*

But a bigger betrayal hits as the question swirls: Did my mother fake her own death? When she went into hiding, she also hid from me, her only daughter. If she's alive today, she must know about Dad. She would know the virus killed him, leaving me completely alone. If she didn't come out of the woodwork then, when Dad's death tore me apart in ways that will never heal, I doubt she ever will.

"That's where you're wrong," I tell Flower, a terrible sadness filling me. "If she wants the world to believe she's dead, she wants me to believe it too. She won't come looking for me."

Flower's shoulders slump as her gaze drifts to the table full of paper.

Brock shifts into action mode. "We're going to set up a security cam outside your shop. And bug your apartment, if you allow it."

"No," I say, kneejerk. "Don't do any of that. It's not worth it. Trust me."

Flower looks pained. "Chevy, it's your *mother*—"

"Yeah, and if she's not dead, well...she's dead to me."

CHAPTER 21

The city's still in lockdown. The streets feel like an old Western black-and-white film. My driverless cab deposits me in front of my shop, and I fight a twinge of abandonment.

I barely remember leaving the station after arguing until blue-faced with Brock to hold off on installing cameras and mics in my living space. I won that battle—for now. My life won't yet be under a microscope, every motion examined by the Feds. But part of me wonders if it would make me feel less alone.

Standing on the curb as the cab zooms off, I feel rooted to the spot. The wind stings my eyes as I scan my familiar block, which is bare and depressing. Even the homeless woman's nook is empty. The newspapers have blown away to reveal a dark patch with a forgotten, crumpled, wool blanket. A smidge of me wonders where she might be.

I step heavily into my shop and peel off my mask. A wave of apathy blankets me as I consider whether my mother might still be alive. Seriously, Special Agent Flower? My mother's been in hiding, and may—likely *not*—come find me? Even if it were true, I couldn't care less.

There's only one thing I care about right now. Gage.

The alien light shines like a spotlight on him, and it seems to highlight the mechanics hiding beneath his skin. I shut off the light, and the room goes dusk as gray light filters in through the window.

I slink onto the floor beside Gage, who is blanketed in shadow, with only a hint of his features visible. When I touch his hair, his head tips back like it's on a hinge. His jaw goes slack. A sob chokes out of me without warning.

"Gage, babe. Please." I'm a blubbering mess. "I need you to come back to me. I need you now. No more of this sleep-mode bull-crap."

I collapse onto his chest, which is rigid with cold.

"I need you back. And I need you to tell me what to do. I need your help. Please, Gage. Please."

Snot and drool swamp my face. My tear ducts are like twin faucets that can't shut off.

Gage is gone. I cry desperately for him. My father is gone. A wracking sob escapes, I miss him so much. My mother is gone but still haunts me. Am I crying for her? Only angry tears.

Self-pity is there too. I cry for me. Pathetic, heartbroken, wallowing me. It's a flood of unhinged emotion.

I rip myself from Gage and crawl toward my work table, which is covered with shiny new jewelry pieces. The sight of them depresses me more.

Somehow, I manage to get upstairs. My apartment feels neglected and dusty, but it's home. My apartment's familiar scent is a comfort—pistachios and jasmine tea. After a bowl of leftover pasta, I shower and fall into bed. Weighed down in the inky darkness, my body sinks into the mattress. When was the last time I slept? A fleeting thought.

Sleep comes hard. And long. And dreamless.

THE CLOCK READS 2:24 when I come to. In my hazy waking moments, I think I've only slept an hour. But daylight tells me it's after two in the *afternoon*. I've slept over twelve hours. My body reluctantly follows my brain's orders to start moving. My legs shift off the bed.

The bathroom mirror shows a war-torn Chevy. My curls are

matted to my head. My eyes are puffy. Running water on cold, I mop my face with it. The shock is welcome.

Another shock, not so much.

A splash of red, like bright paint, on toilet paper pulls me into full consciousness. I got my period? That's weird. I'm not due for another—

Wait—what day is it?

After dealing with the blood, I check the calendar on my Ping. What the—?

Something plummets inside me, and I rail silently at myself. I've made another mistake. This one, huge.

My weekly Vax.

I missed it.

How could I let that happen?

No doubt I've been distracted. Still, this Vax is my *lifeline*. Heat fills my body, crawling up my neck. Frantic, I search for the light blue tub that holds our Tylenol and cough syrup and Vax stash. But Gage is the one who administered my Vax each week. He knows where this stuff is. He'd been in charge of renewing monthly shipments, having worked at Vexxe and being on the front line of worldwide distribution. I have no idea what I'm doing.

A tingly feeling creeps down my arms as I realize how much control I'd relinquished to him, how thoroughly I had buried myself under a rock. Of all the signals that should have been a warning—like stumbling on my Partner Stats—missing my Vax is like a slap in the face. How irresponsible, relying on a droid to keep me alive. Emotions choke me, thinking of my Gage that way. I shake it off and focus on the task at hand. I need to inject myself. Now.

With shaky hands, I fill the syringe, uncertainty coating me in a tepid sweat. I realize with dread that I've never given myself a shot before. Is my arm the best spot, like Gage always did? Or do I go for my thigh? *Argh*, no time to waste. I stab the needle in my leg, wincing as the miracle juice goes in.

One dose closer to my last.

My heart races. I throw the empty needle into the sink. My face falls into my hands. Am I really this helpless?

Come on, Chevy. Be strong! Get your head clear.

Think. What will happen when I run out of Vax? Will my fate match Dad's? Will I contract the dreaded virus and die a painful death? It's been a couple years since this virus has been a threat. Has it weakened? Have we built up a herd immunity? If I'm at risk, that means each Vexxe customer—worldwide—is at risk. Is that what these hack-ware jerks were hoping? To wipe us all out?

A shudder runs through me. Time is running out. I've got to figure out a way to get more Vax. But I can't do it alone. I need help.

I circle my kitchen island, thoughts throbbing like tooth pain. Who could possibly help with this? Brock and Flower? No. I refuse to buy into their ridiculous theory that my mother faked her death and is still alive somewhere, lurking in the shadows. And I refuse to help them in their witch hunt to find her.

Gosh, I wish Dad were still here.

Zara and Tig? The lovebirds? Do they realize what's at stake, or are they too much in the love zone to take notice?

Shame on you, Chevy. They could've said the same about you and Gage.

Lederhorn? He's more than a mechanic. A survivor, his first words to me come back—*I had an everything too.* He must have been speaking about a lost love.

I Ping the clinic. No answer. Either they're closed or following the device shutdown orders. Probably the latter. Like hospitals, they can't afford to be closed in times of crisis. I'll have to physically go there and find him.

After throwing on some clothes, I fluff my curls and mask up. Rain taps on the window glass. Clicky sounds tell me it's icy. My bright yellow umbrella will draw too much attention, so I pull my hood over my baseball cap before heading out. As I step onto the sidewalk, sleet pelts my mask.

Uncertainty makes me pause. Action needs to be taken, but am I being reckless right now? The city's in lockdown...

The eerie stillness of the city feels like a weight on my shoulders. How long do I stand there, in front of my shop, stuck in a limbo of hesitation?

While concentrating on the cement beneath my boots, I visualize the earth beneath and the fiery core at its center. I inhale a mouthful of mask, and what's left of my energy crashes.

My legs can't seem to move. That flat apathy comes over me again. There is another option—to stop fighting. To accept my fate, whatever it may be. Maybe my fate is to join Dad on the other side.

Can't save everyone, right Doc?

That includes me.

My movements are slow as I turn back to go inside. I have some time left. A few weeks? Maybe a month? I'll spend it doing what I love to do, and focus on my art.

A resigned relief makes me breathe easier now, even as my key sticks in the lock. As I jiggle it loose, I spy none other than the homeless woman in her usual spot. Feeling as if I have nothing to lose, I go to her. Her shivering figure shrinks under the wet wool blanket.

"Ma'am? Come with me. Let's get you warm and dry." A bolt of energy fills me as I say the words.

But the woman doesn't move. She keeps her head downturned. All I can see is her grubby baseball cap.

"Ma'am? Did you hear me? It's not safe to be out. There's a lockdown. My apartment is right over there."

She shakes her head ever so slightly. The movement seems vulnerable and sad and makes me want to help her more.

"You'd be doing me a favor, really. I could use some company right about now. It's been a brutal few days."

The cap tips upward, and her eyes beneath the rim meet mine. She goes as still as the city around us. I pause, unsure. She seems familiar, but not.

She's not wearing her signature glasses.

"Chevy," she says, a world of apology in it.

I freeze, the blood in my veins stopping dead, yet burn through my skin.

I won't call her Mom. I refuse to call her Mom.

"Doc?"

CHAPTER 22

There's a volcano of anger inside me. Before she can respond—my undead, in-hiding, homeless mother—I spin back and work the sticky lock. Why the heck didn't I convert to e-locks years ago? Steam rises from my collar as I break out in a nervous sweat. I mumble a curse under my mask, hoping Doc hears it.

"Chevy."

She's right behind me now. Too close. I flick a glare in her direction. She cowers beneath the dirty blanket she wears like a cape. It smells like city garbage, and I feel a flare of disgust. "Sorry," I snap. "That invitation was meant for someone else."

"Chevy, please. We need to talk."

Finally, my key works. I hurry in and let the door shut. But she holds it open, her face a picture of agony like I'm torturing her.

"Where's your mask?" I blurt as if I'm the mother. "I gave you one. Where is it?" As soon as I say it, regret stings. Why do I care? In the big picture of how my mother has wronged me, this is small potatoes. Like, minuscule.

She offers a patronizing smile. "Can I come in?"

Argh. Another buzz of anger. Why does she affect me like this?

"Whatever. I don't care."

But as I pivot away, my body knots up inside. I *do* care. And that pisses me off. Each stair to my home seems like a test. My boots stomp hard to drown out her footsteps following. A million questions flood my brain, but I'm too annoyed to heed them.

And then, she's standing in my kitchen, which triggers a surreal nightmare-like moment. It's dizzying. I want to scream. How is my dead mother standing here in my apartment?

She glances around as if taking inventory, and hugs that skanky blanket to her shoulders. My apartment fills with garbage stench. "This is where you live," she says, still with that condescending grin.

"Yeah, no kidding. You've known I live here. How long have you been spying on me?"

Her face changes, a weariness tugging at it. "Oh, Chevy, please. Let's sit and talk like civilized adults."

"Ha! You want to sit and *talk*?"

Her body trembles beneath her blanket. "Would it be too much to ask for some tea? I'm freezing."

"I bet you are. It's ridiculous out there." I flick a hand toward the window. "It's crazy that you've been hunkering in a doorway like a homeless person all this time when—"

A clogging in my throat cuts me off. Grabbing the kettle, I brusquely fill it with water and slam it on the burner. I turn on the gas like it's an old-timey radio dial. I grab mugs, tea bags, and honey like I'm on autopilot. *What the hell am I doing?* So many questions. So much resentment. There is zero chance I can sit and have tea without confronting her.

"You left me."

"Can I sit?"

I gesture to a kitchen stool. She moves wearily as if suffering from chronic pain, and concern comes over me. I turn away before a tear escapes. Leaving her in my kitchen without a word, I charge into the bathroom in hopes for a reset.

Avoiding my reflection, I dab my eyelids with cool water. Doc's picture is still wedged in the mirror—the professional headshot that had been splashed all over the news. Once the most recognizable faces in the country, it's a complete diversion from the living, breathing human in my kitchen with a grimy blanket and frizzy curls and tired, glasses-free eyes.

Snatching up the photo, I study it, irrationally hoping this is not my mother. Do we share any resemblance? We have the same pointy chin. In her disheveled appearance, I'm reminded we have the same wild tangle of curls.

The kettle's whistle builds to a scream before I'm out. Glad for the task, I fill the mugs and swirl the honey. Taking a seat at the island, I stare at the darkening liquid in my cup, numb with shock.

"Thank you," she says softly.

Her glasses are back, and the effect is instantaneous. Like a magic trick, she's Doc. And at once, her presence is easier to categorize. Emotion is taken out of this whole situation. I can't stop staring at her, disbelief nagging like a leaky faucet.

"I have to be careful with these glasses," she says. "They are too recognizable. But I have to admit, I'm almost blind without them."

In no mood for small talk, I slurp my tea—and wince in pain. It's blistering hot.

"Better blow on it first," she says.

A fire ignites in me. "I don't need you to school me in the art of tea drinking, thank you very much."

She blinks at me, her expression neutral. "Sorry."

Part of me wants her to reprimand me. Be a mom, for once.

She cocks her head. "I owe you an explanation."

Such a major understatement, it's absurd. A gurgling starts low in my belly and comes out as bitter laughter.

"They went after me, Chevy. It was terrifying. I had to do something. They tried to *kidnap* me. Who knows where I could've ended up? Maybe in some kind of underground drug-ring compound where I would be forced to cook up dose after dose of vaccine...like one of those meth kitchens."

I return her blank stare.

"Are you hearing me?" she says.

"I hear you. But you got away from them? I mean, you didn't get kidnapped, right?"

She drops her chin to her chest. "It wasn't easy."

"So, what then? You ran away? Went into hiding? Right outside of my apartment?"

"Not exactly—"

"That's rich, Doc. I mean, what kind of brainiac thought up that scheme?"

She lets out a sigh. "It would help if you would at least try to be a bit more empathetic."

"Huh." I bite my lip against impudence.

"I am your mother, after all."

The fire comes roaring back. I'm on my feet. "Oh? I think that's up for debate right now, considering everyone—including me—has believed you were dead for the past two years."

"I know. It's been a long time."

I hug myself tight, but it doesn't contain my anger. "Two years is nothing. Long before that, I'd grown used to *not* having a mother."

Her face goes pale. "That's a cruel thing to say."

A tense silence descends. I fill my mouth with a gulp of tea to stop the string of cruelty itching to come out. But I refuse to apologize.

"Chevy, I know you're angry. You have every right to be—"

"You know Dad died, right? You had to have known that."

She stares at her dirt-rimmed fingernails. "Yes, I knew he was sick. And I knew he lost his battle with the virus."

The steaming tea does little to soothe the jumble in my chest. "And you didn't think to find me? You didn't think I might need some kind of parental *something* to help me through that?"

"It was too soon. I-I couldn't risk—"

"I, I, I," I mock. "That's the problem. It was always about *you*."

"That's not fair. Nor is it true, and you know it. I spent my whole career saving people's lives—"

"And ignoring your family."

"Chevy."

"What?" I hate to hear my name from her lips. She has no right to it. My *father* named me. "Could you have saved Dad?" I screw up my face at her, knowing the answer. "You were the vaccine queen. You could've saved him, am I right?"

She looks pained. "It's not that simple."

"Yes or no. Seems simple enough."

Her gaze finds the window. Icy rain still pelts the glass. "I couldn't say."

I throw up my hands. "What do you mean?"

"As you must know by now, the virus was more deadly in males than females. Looking at the survivor data, we find fewer surviving men than women."

"Okay..."

"So, the vaccine seems to fully protect women."

"And not Dad?"

"And not *men.* Remember the federal push to maximize cryobanks and sperm banks to maintain future populations? There are so few men left that the viability of the human race is at risk. We were still working on modifying the serum for the Y chromosome, sensing that..."

Her words trail off as images flash in my memory. Boys from my childhood, my high school, disappeared one by one, dying before the sickness took hold. The first was so tragic—Timber Hobbs, who taught me how to roll the perfect snowball in third grade. I refused to believe he was gone. By the time the deaths became commonplace, boy after boy, I had become practiced in my ignorance. With my blinders firmly in place, I went about custom-ordering my own personal droid-partner, Gage. And then I stopped noticing altogether.

But now, I can't help but notice unmasked faces are everywhere. Squat-smock, bearded cabbie, bank security. *What model are you?* All droids. All men. And then there's Lederhorn, an old man, one of the rare survivors. And there in his repair clinic, he's surrounded by droids. There are hardly any female droids.

What did I care? I had my Gage, and that's all I needed.

Thoughts of Gage surge to the forefront, unbidden, and guilt stabs. He's downstairs, still in sleep mode—a holding pattern. A fierce protectiveness layers over the guilt and yearning, and I promise to keep his existence a secret from my mother.

I interrupt her dissertation. "I could report you to the Feds, you know. They're looking for you. They know you're alive."

That stops her. She eyes me with measured fear.

"But I won't," I tell her, though I'm not sure why. "Not yet, anyway."

"Thank you." She sounds overcome with fatigue suddenly. Her mug trembles as she lifts it to her lips. "Would it be possible...would you mind if..."

"What?"

"A bath would be heaven right now."

I feel myself smile, in spite of everything. "I bet."

CHAPTER 23

Soon after my mother disappears into the bathroom, steam from her bath creeps through the door crack, and makes my place feel warmer and more lived in. Some of those hard knots inside me dissolve.

It triggers a manic energy within me. And a cleaning frenzy. I scrub the kitchen until it's sparkling. I zap dust mites from the living area. I freshen the rugs with a thorough vacuuming.

Symbolic? Maybe. What I need is a spiritual cleansing. A new beginning. But I'm not sure that's happening.

Out the window, the icy rain has shifted to a blustery squall. Part of me feels relieved that my mother is safe indoors, in my home.

Another part of me cannot climb over my resentment toward her. It's deep. Like, cavernous. *She didn't die. She abandoned me.* The shock of this discovery is still fresh. And it stings over and over like I'm trapped in a bee's hive.

By the time Doc emerges aglow from her bath, the apartment is spotless. She wanders around, studying little artifacts of my life scattered throughout my place—ubiquitous stuff I don't see anymore. Now it feels cramped, like her presence has infected the air. Out of a pure need to keep busy, I haul out the flour to make bread, messing up my newly cleaned kitchen.

Small sacrifice.

"Who lives here with you?" Her back is turned so I can't see her face, but her concerned tone makes me go rigid.

"No one. Why?" She has no right to Gage. Any part of him.

She shows her pinched profile. In her hands is a framed picture of me and Dad. "You miss him, don't you?"

My throat fills. "I don't want to talk about it."

Eventually, she settles on a kitchen stool. "Who taught you how to make bread?"

Gage.

I shrug and say nothing.

She hugs herself and exhales. "Chevy, I need your help."

My frown is automatic. She wants more help? As if hiding her from the Feds isn't enough?

"I know about Vexxe," she says. "I know about the hack-ware attack that's caused the nationwide shutdown."

I eye her warily. Does she know about Gage? That they got to Vexxe through him? My conscience spirals with guilt. Does she know about the ransom? Does she know I almost squandered my entire inheritance trying to save him?

But the scolding doesn't come. "There's a reason they're looking for me. Not just the Feds, but the hack-ware terrorists as well."

So, she knows they attacked Vexxe to get to her. There's a sticky pause until I hold her gaze.

She palms the counter. "We need a new vaccine. The virus has mutated. This attack and the shutdown? It's a reactionary response. People are panicking. But science shows that even without the attack, we'd be in trouble right now."

Her words reverberate in my skull: *The virus has mutated.* "What do you mean, in trouble?"

"The new variant of the virus is dangerous, and it needs to be mitigated. With a new vaccine."

New variant? Does that mean…?

On Mondays, Gage would inject my weekly Vax to keep me alive. It had been our routine. And it kept me safe, I thought. "Are you telling me the Vax I've been taking every week isn't effective anymore?"

"No, it is. It's probably at 40% efficacy by now."

Heat shoots down my leg, stemming from where I'd stuck in the Vax hours ago. A Vax that's basically ineffective. "You can't be serious."

"We knew the vaccine was a first-phase. We fully anticipated modifying the formula to address the variants. But then..."

"You disappeared."

Her gaze hardens. "Chevy, my team was killed. My entire team at the lab—picked off one by one. They made it look like fluke accidents. But quickly, I realized these were no accidents."

"What do you mean they were *killed*? Didn't the virus take them?"

She shakes her head. "That's what they wanted the public to believe. We had been testing on ourselves as our trial subjects dwindled. But medically, we were safe. Very safe. Truthfully? My team and I had built up antibodies so that we didn't need the weekly vaccine."

Irrationally, I'm annoyed that she's got antibodies while the rest of us must rely on medicine to stay alive. "That's why you don't wear a mask? That's why you didn't wear the one I gave you?"

"I wore it sometimes. But not for protection." A smile rises. "It helped disguise me."

My fists clench bread dough. "How did you know you were in trouble? And how did you get away?"

"When Mandee, my assistant, was struck with the virus, they sent a replacement. But she wasn't a nurse or a scientist or even a graduate student intern. This woman—she was middle-aged and sharp as a tack. She knew things before coming on the job that no layperson could possibly know. But her resume was filled with odd jobs, showing no relevant experience. It didn't match up."

"Sounds scary."

She ignores my sarcasm. "One night, I went back to the lab after a late meeting. And there she was, in my work area. I have no idea how she got in there. I'm always careful to lock up." She wrings her hands.

"What was she doing?"

"Messing with the vials. Trying to poison me."

I unleash an eyeroll that had been itching to come out. "Come on. That sounds paranoid."

"It would if it didn't happen to my colleagues."

"They were poisoned?"

"As I said, we'd been testing on ourselves. The next day, two others on my team were struck down—dead—hours after injecting themselves."

This news makes me squirm with discomfort. It's hard to wrap my head around. "So, you ran."

"No. I faked illness. I got admitted as a patient. And then I ran."

I put the blob of dough into the preheated oven, and then slam the door shut. "Why are you telling me this? It doesn't matter. It's done. It's in the past. I don't want to hear that you're sorry, and I don't want to tell you it's okay. It's just...what it is. Let's move on. You're here. You're alive. And you're sitting in my apartment." I pull at my curls, trying to process what's happening. My mother is here, alive...

Something nags at me. Why is she exposing herself now?

"You obviously need something from me," I say. My next words are forced. "How can I help?"

The air tenses in the room. "I need a lab."

"You need a *lab?*" My next thought is silent: And how am I supposed to help you find one?

"Yes, a safe space to create a new vaccine. Not the hospital, obviously. Someplace hidden," she says, her gaze pinned on my butcher block counter that's dusted with flour. She taps some on her finger and blows it off like fairy dust. "And it can't be your kitchen."

A safe space to create a new vaccine.

My studio? The thought vaporizes in a second. No way. It's not hidden enough. Besides, it's *my* space. And Gage is there, waiting for—

My Ping buzzes. Zara.

"I have to take this." After closing myself into my bedroom, I whisper, "Zara, hey."

There's so much to say, but I can't blurt it out. *My mom is here, alive, hiding from the Feds and the hack-ware jerks...* Everything in me wants to tell her. But what if the Feds are tracing my Ping? It's almost certain they are. Technology was made for spying—in disguise as customer service.

"Are you okay?" she says. "You sound weird."

"I am weird."

It's good to hear her laugh. "Very true. Okay, listen. I'm not liking the idea that you're alone right now. Isolation can do scary things to someone's psyche. What if Tig and I come over? They lifted the lockdown temporarily, so we can stay with you until eight tonight. Or you'll have houseguests for the indefinite future. Ha!"

Ha, is right. If she only knew I already have a houseguest.

"Oh," I manage.

"*Oh?*" she mocks. "Does that mean you want us to come? It's still a blizzard out there, but we can get there if you want."

"Um." As much as I don't want to admit it, everything's changed since Doc came on the scene. "Maybe don't come, then."

"Chevy? What's going on?"

Oh, man. I so want to tell her. "How is your Vax stash?" I ask instead.

"Dwindling. But, whatever."

"You're not worried?"

"Tig and I decided we won't worry. It won't do any good. We'll just hope and pray we don't get sick. And be careful."

I'm tempted to tell her what I've learned—that the vaccine we thought kept us alive is only 40% effective. "You should probably stay home."

"Okay," she says. "We'll stay put. But call when you need me. Or if you change your mind. Anytime."

"I will."

We disconnect, and a triumphant feeling lifts me, sensing I evaded a trap from the Feds. Who knows if I did? And at some point,

I might need their help. But right now, I need to figure out what to do with Doc.

And how to get more vaccine.

Two for one—I have an idea.

CHAPTER 24

Like a statue at the kitchen island, Doc hasn't moved since I took Zara's call. I duck into the bathroom, which is still humid from her bath. A shower will help me noodle out my plan to find a makeshift lab for Doc to create a new vaccine.

My idea? The repair clinic. It's a perfect place for a secret lab—sanitary, discreet, and equipped with tools. Lathering shampoo into my curls, I serve up a silent apology. Lederhorn doesn't want to be dragged into this mess, but the clinic may be our only option.

I disable my Ping after getting dressed to block any chance of Brock and Flower finding us. It also prevents me from reaching Lederhorn. Such a circuitous day. Before Doc found me, I had been on my way to see him. Now, I'm bringing her along.

Skipping the blow-dryer, I cover my wet hair with a knit hat. Boots, coat. Outside is still a blizzard. Good. Better for hiding en route.

"I have an idea," I call to Doc from my bedroom. "I know where to take you."

No answer. Where's Doc?

My apartment's empty. It smells like a bakery. I spritz the bread with water and shut off the oven. I circle the perimeter of my living area as if she's hiding.

"Doc?"

Is she out on the cold streets already? Gage's winter jacket is missing. She must be outside.

"Silly goose," I say aloud, the moniker she used for me when I was little.

I race down the stairs, a reprimand forming on my lips. Out the window, she's nowhere to be seen.

My studio?

My stomach plunges as I push open my studio door.

Smack in the middle of the room, with hands on hips, she hovers over my Gage like a predatory hawk. The sight sends a shiver through me.

"Ready? Let's go," I say.

Doc's voice is tinged with disgust. "What is this, Chevy?"

Bitterness rises like bile. "Never mind. Don't you need your secret lab? I'm ready to take you."

She shows her profile, not meeting my eye. "Is it yours? This droid?"

Her tone makes me bristle. "No. I mean, yes." My studio feels crowded now. "It's none of your business."

She cranes to study his face—his flawless, beautiful face. "I recognize it."

Not it, *him*. "No, you don't."

"I've seen it walking the block. I've seen it enter this building. It stays with you, upstairs."

Irritation needles me. "Stop calling him *it*, okay? His name is Gage."

Her snicker is like nails on a chalkboard. "His name is Gage," she parrots, and her mocking tone cuts into my heart.

A roiling heat builds in my veins, and rises like smoke up a chimney. *Get out*, I want to scream.

She caresses the lapel of the jacket she wears. "This is his coat, then?"

"Yes." A sob erupts with the word, and I lean down to brush back Gage's golden hair. Swallowing my tears, I use a forceful tone. "He saved me. Since Dad died, he's been my only happiness. I'm not letting you take that from me."

"Oh, Chevy." Is it pity in her tone now?

"I don't want to hear anything from you. I don't need a lecture. I certainly don't need your permission. For anything."

Her eyes soften. "Of course, you don't. You are a strong, independent woman."

I turn on her. "How would you know?"

"Chevy, you're my daughter."

"You hid from me. You left me all alone."

"You weren't alone. Your father—"

"Died. And still, you hid."

"Zara—"

"Don't you dare use Zara to justify what you did. She's my forever friend. She would never abandon me. She and Gage got me through..." My words trail off. I turn away, unable to face her now. "I'm not strong."

The admission is like therapy. I want to be strong. But I'm not. I'm a mess without Gage, without Zara, without Dad. I've buried myself in grief, but Gage gave me comfort and healing. He is my strength.

Doc's hands on my shoulders feel sharp and cool, like sloth nails. "I'm sorry I wasn't there for you. I'm glad you had Gage to help you through."

Her words surprise me, but I don't let her see it.

"I'm no expert on droids. But I think that was the concept behind the invention. They were built to help us survivors feel less alone. Some may see it as a crutch, but I don't. I think it was smart of you— using a droid for the purpose for which they were built. Good job."

Now I do face her, squinting in disbelief. She talks like Gage is a freaking toaster and has the nerve to congratulate me for using it.

She zips Gage's jacket up to her chin. "But you also don't want to grow too dependent on them. Emotionally, you know."

Her words make my skin prickle, a harsh truth there. "I'm not. Don't worry." I don my mask like it's armor. "You still need a secret lab, yeah? Let's go."

CHAPTER
25

We take the subway to the repair clinic, using separate trains in case the Feds are trailing us. Doc's disguise seems so lame. Now that she's been exposed, she's easily recognizable. Or maybe it's our bond of blood that makes it obvious to me.

Hiding out for the past two years has given Doc skills in being discreet. She doesn't miss a beat—so sneaky, she's practically invisible.

As planned, I get off one stop before she does and walk the few blocks to meet her. Tucked inside a building's alcove, I think of the homeless woman I took her for. An ache goes through me. How did she feel as she hid in plain sight on the street near my apartment? Cold and lonely. What did she do all day, aside from trying to keep warm? Fresh tears sting my eyes. This is my *mother* who was out on the streets, while I stayed warm and oblivious in my snug apartment. My heart breaks to imagine it.

I zone in on the steam emitting from the subway stop, hyper-aware of the tension that builds in my body. She should be here by now. Where is she? Worry ripples through me as minutes tick by. Still, no sign of her. Have the Feds found her?

Eventually, a few commuters exit the station in a slow trickle. My eyes burn watching for Doc. Until an opposing figure emerges out of the mist like an apparition, and gives me pause. An ominous shadow —tall and broad, in dark clothing. A man. Maskless. A droid?

He pauses at the top of the stairs, head swiveling back and forth.

I duck into the alcove and out of sight. When I dare to peek again, he's moved to the other side of the railing—a spot hidden from anyone coming up.

A gust of panic compresses my chest. Is this the Feds? Did they send a droid to get her?

A voice echoes faintly in the empty street. It's coming from the droid, but his lips aren't moving. It's his internal speaker; he's receiving a message. My ears get huge as I try to make it out. When it ends, he taps his ear and answers.

In a foreign tongue.

Oh, no. These aren't US droids.

Fear replaces panic. My blood feels like it's riddled with thorns.

A black van pulls up to the curb near the subway stop and the droid nods to the driver. Clearly, they are on the same team. I try to make out the license plate on the van, but its digits are smudged. The van itself looks like it came from a junkyard, full of dents and rust. Tailpipe emissions waft, ominous, like a simmering bomb.

These can't be the Feds. This is not a government vehicle. Are these the hack-ware jerks? The Russian mafia?

My pulse races, but I'm frozen still. Sweat gathers under my hat. The next few seconds feel like a year.

When Doc finally emerges from the subway fog, regret and fear and panic tornado in my chest.

I watch in horror as the droid lurches toward her.

Holy crap!

A strangled sound erupts from me. He's going to throw her in that van. To kidnap her?

I jump out onto the sidewalk, tearing my mask away. "Doc! Run!"

We lock eyes for a millisecond. The droid follows her gaze.

Before he reacts, she breaks into a sprint toward me.

I fall into step beside her, and we take off side by side.

"Droid. Foreign," I chant between puffs of air.

Doc runs harder.

Droid footsteps drumroll behind us. Right on our heels. He's fast.

As we round the corner, Doc swipes off her cap. We swap, and it's like we share a brain. Will this be enough to confuse them?

Doc is winded. Her stride falters.

Come on. We can't afford the slightest misstep.

"Bring him around," she says, and ducks into an alley.

Bring who around? The droid?

But Doc's gone.

Inertia pushes me forward. Doc abandoned me. Again. Is she giving me up to these guys? She couldn't outrun them but neither can I. Or can I?

Fear and adrenaline give me superhuman speed. I pump my arms to propel myself forward.

The screech of tires mutes out the droid's footsteps. Diesel fumes cloud the air. It may be a clunker but it's impossible to outrun. I need to outsmart it.

I round the corner—taking a left turn. Easier on foot than in a vehicle. It buys me a few more seconds. I race through a crosswalk and pray the traffic light turns red.

Doesn't matter.

Tires scream through the red light. The van revs, bearing down. It's too close. My heart gallops faster than I can run.

The van is right next to me, decelerating to track me. The driver yells, his words alien. In my periphery, I see him. Another foreign droid.

In the passenger seat, someone else. A woman? I peek again. It's a stocky brunette wearing a mask. Officer Brock?

No way. I reject the thought. These aren't the Feds. These aren't police.

The van's wheels climb onto the curb.

Oh no—it's going to run me down.

Sidestepping close to the buildings, I duck under scaffolding and pray it doesn't collapse on top of me.

The van inches closer, kicking up dirt with its tires. I blink sand out of my eyes. It's like I'm trapped inside a tornado.

Tiny stones make my boots slip. Ahead, the scaffolding ends—light at the end of a tunnel. I fly out, toward the light. And in the open sidewalk, I see it.

Bring him around. I know what Doc meant. I power to the other end of the alleyway.

Doc's alley. She's there!

Midway down, she flails her arms in big sweeping arcs. *Hurry, hurry!*

A big feeling rises. She didn't abandon me after all.

I charge down the narrow alley with lightning on my feet.

The van's engine grows distant. The stench of trash and urine and grime replace the odor of diesel. Another sound, the distant, low snarl of wild dogs, makes me cringe. Tires screech to a halt. The alley is too narrow for the van to fit through.

Doc directs me up a fire escape ladder. I scale it, and squeeze through a broken window, dodging the sharp glass.

Doc, behind me, pauses at the top of the fire escape. She kicks at the ladder's rotting hinges over and over. The rust finally gives way. The ladder breaks off and swoons to the ground like a fallen tree.

She pushes past the jagged glass, ripping Gage's jacket. We huddle inside, staring out, our panting in sync like prayer.

For an eerie moment, everything is quiet.

But not for long.

At the end of the alley, van doors open. Voices echo. Two men call to each other in a strange language.

The drumroll of droid footfalls come closer, into the alley. I hold my breath and watch them pass the fallen ladder. They pass our window. They run by an open manhole, an overflowing dumpster...

And then they're out of sight.

My heart beats wildly. Where are they? Will they find us here?

I turn to Doc, the question on my lips, when a ghastly sound shocks me silent. A noise so disturbing it rocks me to the core.

A cacophony of snarls fills the city gorge.

Wild dogs. Lots of them. Barking. Growling.

They sound like monsters.

An alarm sounds—a droid alert. Then, it warbles out as if a wire is cut.

All city noise is drowned out by the mongrels' howling and snarling. Bile rises into my esophagus, listening.

The dogs make nightmarish sounds I've grown to fear. Since the city emptied out and went black, these mangy hounds have taken over certain parts of the city, creating dens within deserted alleyways.

But, eerily, there's not a single human scream. This, more than the gruesome noise of the growling hounds, chills me to the bone. Brock couldn't be involved in this. No person—no matter how tough —would be able to hold back from screaming in terror while facing those dogs.

"Those dogs...they're ripping the droids to shreds," I whisper.

Doc's breathing is staggered. "That's my hope."

"How did you get past them?"

She holds up her mace. "I pissed them off. They were ready to attack anything that came next."

I swallow down nausea. Terror won't allow any relief. Doc takes my hand, and I hold on for dear life. Thank goodness she's here. Forcing my eyes closed, I guide myself through a few shaky breaths.

Backing away from the window, we take refuge on the floor. Once the shakes stop, I open my eyes to take in our surroundings. We're in a studio apartment that's been long vacated. The bed on the far wall has no sheet or blanket. The couch is overturned. Rodent droppings litter the floor. The funk of animal and mold find my nose. We escaped one hell and entered another. I hug myself, wanting out of this place.

"When will we know it's safe to leave?"

Without answering, Doc goes to the galley kitchen and tries the faucet. When the rusty water runs clear, she drinks.

"Doc, don't drink that water. It's not safe."

"It's never safe, Chevy." She wipes her mouth with Gage's sleeve. "You've got to know that by now."

We squat in the deserted apartment until the streets are silent. Through the broken window, the light changes in the sky. The omnipresent clouds of smog seem aglow. "Must be a full moon," I think aloud.

Doc smiles. "I remember when you could see it."

"Me too. I was little, but I remember. It looked like a shiny dinner plate."

Her smile disappears into a frown. "Those dogs will be hungry. We should find an alternate exit."

"Yeah. Probably soon?" A shudder runs through me, and I'm paralyzed by my fear of the hounds. "Or maybe give them time to move on."

Doc agrees. We move to the bare mattress and huddle there to keep warm. It's one of those blue satin pillow-tops from the olden days. I trace the hourglass stitching with my fingertip.

Doc takes off her glasses. Dirt from her hands smear her cheeks.

In the quiet, the effects of escaping danger and the foreign droids make the bricks between us crumble a bit. "Can I ask you a question?" I say.

"Shoot."

"Did you like being a mother?"

A few beats pass. "You talk as if I'm no longer one."

"No, I mean, did you want to be a mother? Way back when you and Dad were first together?"

"Yes, I think so." She leans against the wall. "Honestly, it's hard to remember. Seems like another lifetime."

"Oh." It's not the answer I expected.

She sighs. "I know you wanted me around more."

Did I want her to be around more? So much resentment fills my childhood memories, it's hard to say. "No, it's not that."

"I could've been better." The sleeves of Gage's coat swish as she folds her arms. "I could have had a more balanced life. I should have been there for you."

The dim light hides my surprise. We're quiet for a while. And in the yawning silence, I feel more of those bricks loosen and fall away.

"Why did you leave me all your money—you know, my inheritance—if you were still alive?"

Her lips curl. "What makes you think it was all my money?"

"It wasn't?"

She pulls a face. "Why would I give you the entirety of my estate? I'm still alive."

"Still. It was a lot of money."

"It is. I had to make it believable. If I left you only a few thousand dollars, it might raise suspicion."

My fingertip is numb from tracing the mattress stitching. It's become a kind of therapy. Or a distraction; I have a hard time making eye contact with Doc. Part of me is still angry she faked her death. Another part is ashamed I almost gave her money away to a bunch of cyber-terrorists. Another tenuous part wonders if I *should* have paid the ransom. But then, a sudden truth smacks: it's not really mine to give.

"I suppose you want that money back, right? I mean, now that at least I know you're alive."

She waits until I look up. "No. No, I don't."

"You don't?"

"It's a gift. For my daughter and only child, whom I love dearly." Her voice sounds like stranger's.

"What did you think... I mean, did you want me to do anything specific with that money? Like, college or something?"

Any dream I had of obtaining a college degree dwindled along with the world's population, thanks to the pandemic. Even if I wanted to go back, there are so few colleges still in existence. Even fewer career choices. What would be the point?

Doc sighs. "I would hope you would be smart with it. Maybe use it to help you find your way."

"Find my way? How?"

"Well, I expect someday you will find a calling. Some way to give back to the earth or help rebuild society. I assume money will be required to get you there."

A familiar, deflated hopelessness crushes me. Though, her pie-in-the-sky ideals for my future shouldn't surprise me. What makes her think I have anything to offer?

At once, I miss the mind-numbing comfort Gage gave me. How simple life seemed when he protected me from its ugliness.

I shrug. "Yeah, well, I'm glad I didn't give it away then."

Doc gives a bark of a laugh. She puts her glasses back on. "You wouldn't give it away!"

I grin through the heat in my face. "You're right. Of course. I wouldn't think of it."

She shakes her head, chuckling. "Come on. Let's get out of here."

CHAPTER
26

The front door of the building makes for a safe exit—away from the hounds in the alley. As we head down the dingy stairwell that's been overtaken by critters and the homeless, I hold my nose against the stench of urine. Out on the street, it feels like midnight, but my Ping tells me it's 5pm. Will Lederhorn still be at the clinic?

Doc and I pull our hoods up and walk in a brisk silence the few blocks to the clinic. I had worried about the Feds, but after that episode with the foreign droids, I'd welcome having the Feds on our tail.

"What is this?" Doc asks when we enter the lobby.

I glance around and see the place through her eyes. It's vast and echoey, an endless industrial gray, dirty and damp. Exposed wires dangle from antiquated light fixtures. Doors are marked with dents and rust. "A repair clinic. For droids."

She scrunches her nose. "It smells like your father."

I smile inside. "Must be why I feel so at home here."

Right now, though, it feels more like a wasteland than home. Doc must feel it too. I lead her to the waiting area, which I had recalled as being warmer, friendlier. But today it feels dank and dusty with no sign of life beyond the vending machine. I do an about-face in search of Lederhorn's office. The sound of our footsteps boom.

"I'm surprised we got in," Doc says. "No one's here."

"Someone's here."

Light peeks out from beneath Lederhorn's office door. I can hear faint music—classical with lots of strings. I think twice before interrupting.

"You should wait in the lobby," I tell Doc. "Let me update my contact here."

Doc backpedals, her brow creased with concern.

I inch the door open. "Mr. Lederhorn?"

The music stops abruptly. Lederhorn stands at the old timey record player with his hand on his heart. "My goodness, child. Are you trying to put me in the grave?" His eyes are smiling but tired.

"Sorry. Didn't mean to scare you. But I need your help. It's urgent." Stepping inside, I'm struck by the warm tones that decorate his cozy office. An aroma of cinnamon wafts, a stark contrast to the sterile warehouse of the clinic.

A bookshelf covers the entirety of one wall, and I'm drawn to the antiquated tombs—books!—like a magnet. My eyes drink in the titles on the colorful spines—*Pride and Prejudice, Moby Dick, The Scarlet Letter, Hamlet, East of Eden, Jane Eyre*—legendary stories from another time. My father once told me these stories were read in school as part of the curriculum before the Department of Education replaced them with texts of history and non-fiction.

"I've never seen so many books before." A chuckle from Lederhorn makes me clarify. "I mean, these kinds of books. Classics."

"I knew what you meant. It's a shame."

"Sorry."

He holds up two fingers. "That's the second time you've apologized in our short time together today. So, what's up, Chevy Rose Davis? How can I help you?"

Hope rises. "You're willing to help?"

He shuffles behind his desk, gesturing for me to sit. His guest chairs are covered with a burnt orange fabric and seem to meld to my body.

Lederhorn tugs off his mask and tosses it on the desk. "I hate that thing. Go ahead and take yours off too. I'm too old to worry about getting that dreaded virus. Besides, I've got antibodies for days."

Dropping my mask feels like lifting a weight from my shoulders.

"Thank you. For everything. How you helped before. Giving me a nudge. It worked. I mean, mostly..."

I give Lederhorn a rundown of what's happened since Gage came home. It's freeing to share details—Tig's pest control efforts and my trip to the police station and report to the Feds. Lederhorn raises his caterpillar brows at the mention of my mother.

On cue, his office door opens, revealing Doc.

Lederhorn comes around his desk. "You must be Dr. Davis."

But Doc's frozen in place, her face fixed in shock as she stares at the old man who's become my friend. I make introductions. "This is Burke Lederhorn, Executive Director of the clinic. Mr. Lederhorn, this is my mother, Dr. Priscilla Davis."

He holds out a hand. "Nice to meet you."

Doc blinks in disbelief. "Incredible."

As Doc and Lederhorn continue their staring contest, I explain why we're here. "My mother needs a safe, secret place to work. To build a vaccine. I didn't believe it was a dangerous mission until we were chased down—"

"You were *chased*?"

"By foreign droids. Probably the same entity that wiped out my lab two years ago," Doc says. "But, now, stakes are higher since the vaccine has lost its efficacy. They're getting desperate. Desperation leads to extreme behavior."

"Even in droids," Lederhorn says. "Whoever controls them, I mean."

"And if whoever controls them knows I'm alive, which it seems they do, I won't be safe until an effective vaccine becomes available. I'll only be safe when they feel they are."

I shrug playfully. "She's hell-bent on saving the world again."

"Well, sure. Sure." Lederhorn scans the clutter on his desk. "You want to do that here?"

"I thought, here in the clinic?" I'm so out of my lane, I'm four-wheeling. "Like, a private room she could use? And you have tools or beakers or whatever?" I appeal silently to Doc—*help me out here*—but she's riveted on the bookcase.

"Oh, my. Look at this. I've never seen so many in one place since...oh gosh, since..."

"Since we had libraries," Lederhorn says.

She offers her small smile, which is less patronizing when directed at him. "Libraries," she echoes.

Libraries. With nostalgia, I recall visiting the grand public places as a young girl before they became overrun by the homeless, before books were deemed too costly to print.

Silence descends as they stare at the wall of books—now artifacts from a lost time.

Doc plucks one from the case. "Here's one for you, Chevy."

It's a thin, white book—the cover is sparse with a sepia image of an ancient man who looks strikingly similar to Burke Lederhorn. In a simple bold script, it reads *Self-Reliance and other Essays* by Ralph Waldo Emerson.

"Read that first one. Self-Reliance."

I take the little book with me as Lederhorn leads us out of his office. "It would be an honor to help in any way I can. Not sure, though, if we have what you need here. This is a repair shop for droids. I'm the only living creature in the building."

Doc straightens. "And the only living male left in the city, more or less."

Lederhorn's laugh is so shy, it's a flirt. "Oh, you flatter me. But yes, that's probably true. More or less."

Back and forth, the two of them. They talk over each other, eager to make a solid plan for whatever medical magic Doc has up her sleeve.

Sheer curiosity has me open the book. "Man is his own star..."

Flipping to the back, I see that this dude Emerson was a Transcendentalist Philosopher. Ah, so that's why we're talking stars. His brain floated among them, clearly. But whoa—a date catches my eye.

"This was written in 1841!" I hurry to catch up to them. "That's like, the time of the dinosaurs."

Doc startles as if she forgot I was there. "It's still relevant."

I frown at the book, mumbling to myself. "It's, like, written in Old English."

Lederhorn brings us to what looks like a surgical room. A single metal table stands in the center. A privacy curtain waits to be unfolded.

"Oh, perfect," Doc says.

"We've made many droids in this room. Years ago. Now the clinic is used mostly to repair those same machines."

Machines. A twitch ripples beneath my skin. He's talking about Gage—and others like him.

Lederhorn pulls out bins of tools and supplies.

"All that's great," Doc says. "But the real magic is within you."

Lederhorn waggles his eyebrows. "Sounds like a Hallmark commercial."

What the hell is a Hallmark commercial?

Doc is all business. "Seriously. You're one of the few remaining male survivors in the city. What has allowed you to survive? The secret may be hiding in your DNA. Would you be willing to give a blood sample?"

Whoa. Doc's request is a shock, certainly a violation of Lederhorn's privacy—the man who wouldn't touch my broken droid for lack of proper insurance. But Lederhorn surprises me.

"Certainly."

"Excellent." Doc lists off the other stuff she needs: needles and syringes and fancy-sounding chemicals that make up medications.

"We'll send Chevy to the pharmacy," he suggests.

"Too risky." Doc shakes her head. "And you're too conspicuous a survivor. You'll draw attention. Can you send a droid? Tech isn't locked down anymore."

That twitch resurfaces. "They can trace droid activity. The Feds, and probably the hack-ware jerks too."

"They can," Doc says. "But they won't know to look. They'll have no reason to be suspicious of a random droid getting common medications from a pharmacy."

"You're right," Lederhorn says. It's like they share a brain. "Good thinking. I'll activate my droid assistant."

Lederhorn leaves, and Doc and I find ourselves alone, together. I tuck into a chair, and open the book I'm grateful to have as a prop. But reading is impossible right now. Especially these long-winded sentences by this Emerson character.

Doc reads over my shoulder and then translates. "Basically, the message is to trust yourself—and *be* yourself—and not conform to what society wants you to be."

"What society? There is no society anymore."

Doc's frown is from grief. "We have a droid-based society."

I slap the book shut as thoughts of Gage hammer into my conscience. How many Gages were there in creation?

Gage felt so human to me, though. It pains me to think of him otherwise, even after the hack, the extended sleep mode, and his sudden absence from my day-to-day. I try to recall his touch, his warmth, his humanness...but it seems far away.

Doc studies me. "The message in *Self-Reliance* could absolutely translate to these times."

"These times, how?" How much of our society is human, and how much is robotic? Can a society sustain itself that way?

Doc seems to have formed her own answers. Her voice is stern. "As a warning not to rely so heavily on droids."

A rush of anger gets me out of my chair. What right does she have to lecture me on how I live my life when she never took an interest in shaping it?

"Or not to rely so heavily on vaccines?" I can't help my snark.

"Chevy," she says in a tone I don't recognize. Disappointed, maybe sad.

As she turns away, regret stings. She's done so much for humankind, including me. Her dedication to the cause came at a sacrifice. She gave up time with her family. Essentially, she gave her life. But now she's here, in the flesh. We have a chance to be a family again. And I'm treating her like the garbage she sat with on the street.

"Sorry, Doc."

To my relief, she offers her hand, and I revel in its warmth. It's a gift to have her back. She's here. She's with me now. I squeeze once, twice, three times—*I love you.*

CHAPTER 27

When Lederhorn returns with Doc's supplies to our makeshift lab inside the repair clinic, my irrelevance paints me beige. I step out of the surgical room without much notice. But where should I go? I could Ping Zara and Tig to try again to fix Gage. But the urgency has left me.

Since Doc discovered Gage, I began to see him differently. Perhaps as she did: a broken machine on my couch. The human element of who Gage was to me, which had felt so real, has faded. And that breaks my heart.

As I wander the clinic, I remember happier times with Gage. On Sundays when the weather was nice, we'd take the train to Coney Island and stroll the beach, visit the carnival artifacts, and imagine the days when lights and music and cotton candy made it a party. Gage didn't need lights and music and cotton candy. He may not have made it a party, but he made it feel normal—even among desolation and neglect, among the bankrupted businesses and shuttered schools. During our excursions, our painful reality fell away. I yearn for those simpler days when we celebrated small beauties. It begs me to wonder, do I miss him or how he made me feel about the world?

I love him. The words are loud in my brain.

"I love him," I say aloud. In the echo, the words boomerang back like a slap in the face. A numbing sadness comes over me.

My steps take me aimlessly around the clinic. I find myself in the big warehouse room where they first put Gage, a repository for defective appliances. Images flood back from that day—Gage lifeless on a hard metal table. Another droid with his chest splayed open, screws and wires and hinges exposed as the mechanic-droid hovered, sparks flying from his giant soldering iron.

The table is cold under my hand. Closing my eyes, I pull in a long breath. Doc was right; this place smells like my father.

And suddenly, there he is, standing on the other side of the table, grinning like the cat who caught the canary.

"How are you, kid?"

"Dad?" This is a mirage, but I don't dare break the spell. "You're here."

As if rising from a dream, we are transported to his workshop in his open garage upstate where car engine innards spot the floor. Relics of my childhood make the dream feel real. Dad plops down in Mom's hand-me-down office chair, the one with duct tape covering the rips in the pleather. He takes a long drink of his fermented ale, his gaze floating to the sky. "You have a job to do in this whole thing, you know. It's not enough to rely on medicine to save the day. Technology is going to play a huge role in getting over this."

My fingertips tingle as his words sink in. He can't be talking about Doc and the vaccine, can he? Gage and the hack-ware attack? He can't know about any of that. He died before any of this happened... This is a *dream*.

"What do you mean, Dad?" I ask cautiously.

His gaze flicks to me. "Your mother will do her part. You have to do yours. The pandemic will never end if the computer virus survives. It's all connected."

He's right. That truth has reared its ugly head—if Vexxe goes down, we all do.

"I know that. But what can I do?" I palm my heart. "I'm just a lovesick girl..."

"Ah, come on. Don't give me that. You're your father's daughter. You fix things. And the vaccine won't save a single soul if the technology can't get it out there."

His words have a paralyzing effect on me. *You're your father's daughter. You fix things.* How does he have that kind of faith in me?

I'm not sure how to respond, but I want to hold him here. Dream or not, I can feel his energy. "Okay," I say finally. "Okay."

We're both quiet for a while. My gaze goes to his latest masterpiece that's appeared as part of this cherished mirage—a shiny new electric engine. My heart cramps with melancholy. The job is done, the hood will close, and the unit will leave this garage, hitting the road to parts unknown, its future as wide as the sky.

"Love you, Dad."

Our eyes meet, and a surge powers through my chest.

He knocks my shoulder with a grease-stained knuckle. "You too, kiddo."

It feels good to laugh. Joy fills me, and I'm as light as air. I sigh to the clouds, happy tears filling. When I blink them away, he's gone.

And just like that, I'm back at the repair clinic, surrounded by sterile chrome tables.

But Dad's essence still lives inside me. I'm my father's daughter.

I can fix things. And I know what I have to do. My heart revs, and I suddenly feel like time's wasting.

CHAPTER
28

I know what to do. I'm my father's daughter. I can fix this!

My staccato steps sound like I'm tap dancing my way back to find Lederhorn, my previous research on how to build computers scrolling in my mind like ticker tape. That research, combined with my programming studies, gives me a killer instinct on the inner workings of computers. I may not be able to undo the virus that's surged into Vexxe, but I can rebuild Gage.

The video app is hot on my tablet—and those instructional videos about how to construct a computer feels like it's built solid muscle memory in me. How droid systems are built, deconstructed, and rebuilt. The similarities to converting combustion engines to electric cannot be a coincidence.

It's as if my father trained me for this very moment. I'm meant to do this work. My tools await at my studio—drill bit, electric flattening mill, soldering iron, sander and file, saw and pliers...

But I need other parts found in this clinic: a new CPU and storage device, RAM for memory, and a PSU for power supply. A new motherboard.

Motherboard.

As I round the corner, the truth swats at my psyche: my mother is alive. A warm tingling fills me, knowing she exists in the world. It's a secure feeling, like there's a safety net beneath the tightrope I'm walking. She's alive...and she's *here*, doing her important work to save humanity.

She's doing her part. And, as Dad said, I have to do mine.

Oh, gosh. My mind's awhirl. There's so much to do—

"Whoa, slow down there."

"Lederhorn! Just the person I'm looking for," I say, winded. "Listen, I need your help."

"Again?" He doesn't break his stride. "I left those supplies with your mother. I think the best thing for us to do is stay out of her way and let her do her thing."

I'm quick on his heels. "Fine. But I'm going to need some supplies too."

He stops and I stumble into his back. "Supplies?"

I tick off my list that's been bouncing around my skull.

He frowns. "Those are parts for—"

"A droid. I know."

He goes still, his eyes question marks.

"Gage's hardware is out of date—ancient—and unable to accept the pest control software. He needs to be deconstructed and rebuilt."

Lederhorn glances toward the surgical wing. "But Tarantula has spread beyond that single droid. It wouldn't make a diff—"

"It will make a difference to me. If nothing else, I'll at least be able to save Gage."

His name echoes in the sterile warehouse. *Gage-age-age-age...* A buried feeling surfaces—is it love? I grasp it like a lifeline.

"Well!" Lederhorn straightens. "I think I know where this is going. If you want to admit Gage here for reconstructive surgery, it would be elective and not covered by insurance. It will be an extremely costly endeavor. It would be more cost-effective for you to purchase a new—"

"No way." He's suggesting I purchase a new droid? As if Gage could be replaced. "Not an option. I don't need your help in that way. No offense."

"No offense taken." He folds his arms. "Tell me, my dear. What do you have in mind, then? What's your plan once you get those parts?"

A spindle of determined energy shoots up my spine. "I'm going to rebuild him myself."

CHAPTER
29

It doesn't take long for my studio to feel like Dad's garage. Memories rise like an unexpected gift, and the day is lost in a beautiful fog of nostalgia...

FROM MY STOOL that felt custom-made for my 12-year-old body, I watched in awe as Dad systematically dismantled the car's innards. Time melted away as Dad's old-timey jams played in the background. He lifted off the car's hood in a grand gesture as if brandishing a shield. Underneath, the maze of tubes and tanks mystified me. For Dad, it was such familiar territory, it was practically home.

Today's project—a compact European model with a stick shift—was one of those jobbies popular for navigating narrow streets of Italy but never caught on in the US, Dad said.

"We like our brute machines on this side of the pond." He sing-songed a sigh. "Even if they destroy the planet."

As he removed its dirty, discarded parts, the apple red bug-like car looked like a go-kart. "When I get old enough," I told him. "I'm going to drive one of these. Fun on wheels."

His power drill paused. "Oh, really? Is that so, Chevy Rose? And how are you going to pay for one of these cherries?"

"You're going to make me one!"

His drill sang to a crescendo as he handed it to me. "Oh no, you're going to have to help. Come on."

The drill felt heavy yet sturdy in my grip. An energy swirled within me. I squeezed the handle like Dad did, testing it out in the air. Easy-peasy.

We're head-to-head over the tangled stuff beneath the hood. Dad pointed with a flashlight. "Next, we take out the radiator."

"What's a radiator do?"

After guiding me with the drill, Dad used a manual screwdriver to remove the radiator and tube. "Keeps everything cool. Engines create a lot of heat."

"You don't need to keep electric cars cool?"

He boings one of my curls. "Smart girl. Yes, you do. We're going to install a different kind."

After a few more amputations, dusty piles filled the corners of the garage, and the car's nose was hollow. Just a frame of red metal now. Would it ever run again?

The track changed to an AC/DC tune as Dad prepared the car lift. Like magic, the car floated into the air. Apple-red color vanished into the heavens, a labyrinth of grimy black pipes in its place.

Dad sent me back to my perch. "Don't want my baby girl getting an oil shower."

"A what?"

As he drained the gearbox and oil, a pungent odor wafted through the garage, deliciously dizzying. If the fumes were a drug, I grew to crave the smell.

Dad muscled through the rest of the car's innards, dislodging chunks of machinery like the suspension and shock absorber. Dad ripped out the engine and set it down. There it lurked, watching us like a hulking bear that's rolled in the dirt. But powerless now. I couldn't tear my eyes from it.

Dad chugged from his water bottle, and the sound made me come to. Dark tear-shaped drops of oil were splattered on his sweatshirt. All his shirts had matching stains, which never came out in the wash. It had been a bone of contention with Mom.

As if we shared the thought, Dad asked, "How's your mother?" The concern in his eyes weren't for Mom, but for me.

"Fine. Working. Always." I couldn't help the bitterness in my tone. "Why can't I live up here with you?"

"You'd miss Zara."

"She could visit. It's only an hour train ride."

Dad wiped his hands with a cloth in a futile attempt to clean them. "I'm working on it, Chevy. Trust me. I want that too." He sounded equal parts determined and sad.

Since the divorce, my life had been split in two. My situation wasn't special, but that didn't make it easy. Every Friday, I took the train to spend weekends with Dad, but it wasn't enough. Weekdays were long and lonely. School only filled a small part of my days. A lot of them were as hollow as this red car's nose.

"Why is it so hard if we both want the same thing?" My question had been on repeat since the separation.

Dad surveyed the car parts and gave his usual answer. "It's a legal thing. A custody thing. The courts decide stuff like that." After a beat, he added, "Divorce is an ugly process."

A dark mass formed in my chest. "I hate it."

"Me too," he said, softer. "I'm sorry."

Sorry. What a weird word. It only made me sadder.

My mind wandered. How did they get together in the first place? Did they ever love each other? My mother and father were such polar opposites, it was a miracle they ever managed to make me, which required two people being pretty intimate. (Yuck to that.) I didn't care if they didn't want each other. But what about me?

I wanted to live here with Dad, not in the empty shell of a home where Mom and I got our stupid mail.

Dad's face was so drawn, I worried he might cry. I shouldn't have brought it up.

My attention turned to the apple-red car. "So, what's next? Can we get to the shiny new electric stuff yet?"

Dad turned on his smile. And it felt like sunshine. "Sure thing, kiddo."

I blink, and I'm in my studio again. My workspace where I used to make jewelry has become an operating table. Gage's body—his *frame* —lies vacant there, his chest cavity emptied. Its innards are spread throughout my studio, much like the piles of car parts in Dad's garage. Led Zeppelin plays in the background in an attempt to channel my father. But without the dust or fumes, Dad feels far away.

So does Gage.

His body is so light, I move him to the couch with ease, and compartmentalize my feelings best I can. He could be an empty apple-red car in need of a smart new engine. His body is a frame now. A lovely, hollow frame soon to be filled with his jibs and jabs and junk that will make him *him* again.

Lederhorn advised me to cover his face while I perform the "surgery." Thank goodness I listened. A sudden chill makes me shiver, and a yearning for Dad comes over me. How I wish he were here right now to help me.

Dad's love had been my strength. Without Gage or my father, I have to find strength within myself.

Be strong, Chevy.

Imagine if the tables were turned. Gage would do anything to save me, even at the risk of his own survival. A fierce determination plays over any concerns now. Failure is not an option. This has to work.

I steel myself against any flimsy sentimentality and refocus. Now that the old—or, as Tig would say, "antiquated"—components are removed from Gage, I can start the rebuild. The video tutorial plays on repeat in my subconscious as I prepare my workspace. I take a deep breath.

First things first—the motherboard.

Motherboard.

The hub, the core, the very component that ties everything together. Lederhorn's words echo from my recon mission to the repair clinic: "The CPU is extremely fragile. See those golden teeth there?

Those are the contacts. Be careful not to touch them. But match up the indicators on the motherboard, and it should fit into place like a puzzle. Voila—the brain and the heart will be able to work together."

The brain and the heart work together.

"Remember," he said, "the CPU is the brain, and the motherboard is the heart."

Mother. Heart.

That's the expectation—a mother's love is a constant, life-affirming force. Why does my own mother's love feel so complicated? Memories of Doc surge. My RAM—random access memory—must be functioning properly, in both speed and performance.

I double check contact points on Gage's new RAM drive as my recollection swirls. Her headshot, as sterile as the hospital that employed her, floats to my mind's eye. But it's quickly swapped with other images I hadn't realized were stored there...

Ten-year-old me padded into my parents' bedroom, which felt bare without Dad, like the engine had been removed. Mom was in bed, awake and working, her laptop propped on a pillow. "I can't sleep, Doc."

Mom's face, lit up from the screen's light, went slack as she removed her glasses. She rubbed her eyes. I froze in the doorway, unused to seeing her vulnerable like this. She blinked at me, her face naked and strange without her severe black glasses. Softer.

She patted the bed beside her. "Come on in." Her rare, gentle tone was like an embrace.

I climbed under the comforter and closed my eyes against the light from her monitor, which cast a warmth into the room. I fell asleep to the tap-tap of her keyboard as if it were music. I felt full, perhaps not with love but with a feeling of safety. Maybe, for Mom, that was the best she could do.

Maybe, for Mom, that was love.

I'M THRUST BACK to the present as if someone slapped me. I blink my studio back into focus.

Lederhorn's voice sounds in my mind, giving me next steps:

"The storage drive plugs directly into the motherboard. And don't forget the IO shield, which protects the motherboard from static and foreign elements like dust. Dust is evil when it comes to these machines."

Dust is evil.

So are viruses.

Fresh ire fills my being. I'm mad at the stars for the existence of viruses. Not just the one that killed my father and took my mother from me...but also Tarantula, the computer virus. I hate it for what it's done to my Gage, my immortal, my sure thing forever. How dare they screw with that.

Viruses have taken everything from me.

My body heats up like a radiator on the fritz. I'm shaking all over. Knowing how precarious my work is, I step away from my workspace. Angry fingers can't meddle with tiny screws and contact points, or fragile, golden teeth. I draw in a shaky breath, and my lungs feel clogged. Maybe a break is in order. Some fresh air? Mentally noting my place like setting a bookmark, I survey the replacement parts— new and clean.

Literally, those shiny new things are my last hope...

"CAN we get to the shiny new electric stuff yet?"

"Sure thing, kiddo."

Dad helped twelve-year-old me off the stool to assist with the final steps of the conversion.

"So, all the electric stuff is going to sit on top of the work-plate, which is like a little table under the hood," Dad said.

Even with more wires in an electric car, it seemed less complicated than the jumble of parts that made up a combustion engine.

"The controller goes here," Dad explained. "And most components plug right into it. Everything has its place, see?"

He guided me to connect fuses and relays. They snapped into place with a satisfying click.

"That's when you know you've done it right." Dad winked. His hand, warm and strong, rested on the small of my back. "There's one thing you have to be extra careful with. You can't forget it, or your electric engine will be ruined."

"The battery?"

"That's important, too. But no. I'm talking about the coolant and pump. To keep things cool."

"Like a radiator?"

"Exactly. All these wires and stuff make a lot of heat. You have to be careful it doesn't burn up. You don't want your insides to melt away. A sad demise, for sure."

A lot of heat.

Keep things cool.

Melt away.

A sad demise.

JUST LIKE THAT, I'm thrust back to the present. Gage's internal computer is an amorphous blob of wire and metal right now—stark and inanimate. A shudder goes through me as I recall Lederhorn's word. Frigid.

It's odd to worry about Gage overheating when he is fixed, going from one extreme to another. It seems wrong to think of him this way, inhuman and mechanical. But the threat of overheating is real.

A pause settles in in my studio with Pink Floyd playing in the background. In slow motion, I go to Gage's frame, his beautiful frame. Those sure arms that used to hold me are now motionless appendages, inactive and numb. Once again, Lederhorn's words come back:

"With traditional computers," Lederhorn explained, "you'd use fans to cool a system. But who would want to hear a fan running inside your droid-partner all day and night?"

He went on when I didn't return his laugh.

"You want to use an all-in-one liquid cooling system. It simply attaches to the motherboard."

Of course she controls the whole band-wagon. How apropos.

My motions are robotic—a defense mechanism—as I complete the final steps in building Gage's computer system. All that's left is his PSU—his rechargeable battery. It's a more compact, cutting-edge version of Dad's electric car battery. It's stupid easy to slide the battery unit into the respective slot. Yet, somehow, it's not as satisfying as clicking the part into place in Dad's garage. This time, the sound feels lonely.

"Done," I announce to no one. Glancing around, I rub my thighs as if to dry off sweat—a nervous habit. Part of me wishes I had done this at Lederhorn's clinic or summoned Tig to help. How am I qualified to do this important job?

Because I'm my father's daughter.

Circling my work table, I study my handiwork. Did I do it right? Only one way to find out.

My finger trembles as I press the power switch. A low humming sound tells me it's working. A vivid, warm energy fills the room. Something releases within me, and I can breathe easier. A swell of pride makes me sit taller.

I did it.

At the couch, I lift the sheet off Gage's lovely face, my heart thumping. There he is, my sleeping beauty, ready to come alive. All I have to do is install the rebuilt computer system into his frame. Easy-peasy, right?

Why am I hesitating? I feel blocked-up inside.

Chevy, stay strong. Gage needs you.

It's true. As much as I might need him, Gage needs me more. And there's still work to be done.

In a weird kind of limbo, I stand in the middle of the room, my arms out like I'm balancing on a paddleboard. On one side is the new engine that will bring Gage life. On the other is Gage—hollow and lifeless.

My hands curl into fists as my eyes squeeze shut. I can't do this alone.

I activate my Ping, chanting as it rings, "Please answer, Zara."

CHAPTER
30

When Zara answers her Ping, her voice is barely recognizable. Is she sick? Or crying?

"Not sick. Not crying," she says drily. "Sleeping. It's one in the morning, Chevy."

Craning toward the front windows, I see how dark and quiet the city is. "It is? Oh." I offer a millisecond of silent apology. "Are you awake now?"

Her yawn sounds like a wind tunnel. "Not exactly."

A zip of urgency runs through me. "Listen, I need Tig to come over and install that pest control software. Gage is ready."

Zara, groggy and hoarse, says, "What do you mean, he's ready?"

My hesitation is unwarranted. So much has happened since I last saw my best friend—the miraculous reappearance of my still-alive mother who must create a new vaccine since our weekly Vax is bogus, the calling from my father to do my part, which led to the heroic reconstruction of Gage's hardware. My instinct is to tell her everything. But right now, we need to focus on bringing Gage back to life. *Keep it simple, Chevy.* "He's been rebuilt."

"You mean his OS has been cleared?"

I circle my worktable and study Gage's new 'engine' from every angle. "No, I didn't touch his OS. His whole system—hardware—has been rebuilt. His CPU and motherboard, all new. The power has been tested, and it works." I glance at Gage and lower my voice as if he's listening. "But it's not in his frame yet, and not hooked into his OS. The pest control needs to—"

"Hold up." Zara seems wide awake now. "Did you take him back to the repair clinic? Did you pay out of pocket? Chevy, this is not—"

"No, no." A laugh flutters out of me. "It's a long story. I got parts from the clinic, but I did it myself."

"You rebuilt your droid yourself?" Zara says, deadpan.

"I did. I'm pretty proud of it, too."

"And Gage's frame is lying empty over there?"

I cringe at her tone. She has good reason to worry, considering my breakdown when he first went into sleep mode. Out the window, the night is a dark, endless black. It seems daylight will never come. I take in Gage's frame on the couch, the white dust protector sheet balled up, exposing a hollow chest cavity. A great sorrow bubbles up inside me. I turn back to my work table, forcing a shaky breath.

"I'm okay," I choke out. "So, can you guys come over? Where's Tig?"

"She's here. Asleep."

They're together. In bed. The realization is like a stab to the heart. "Can you wake her up? This is important."

She sighs. "I know it's important, Chevy. But it's not exactly an emergency."

"It's *not* an emergency?" A few beats pass as my anxiety rises like high tide.

"It's the middle of the night. And we're still in lockdown. If we came now, we'd violate curfew."

I pace the room, jittery. Why can't Zara ignore the rules for once, for me?

Hope slips away and my throat constricts. "I'm all alone, Zara. Please."

"I know. That's why I answered your Ping." She gives a small groan. "Chevy, my dearest friend, can I give you some advice? Cover everything and go upstairs. Get out of your studio for a bit. Eat something. Go to bed."

"But—"

"Remember, we are not droids. For us human folk, sleep and food are fuel. For us, and for you too."

I swallow an icky taste in my mouth. "Okay, boss."

Another sigh. "Tig and I will be there first thing in the morning."

Her words buoy me. "Really? You mean—"

"Of course."

After clicking off my Ping, the truth whacks me hard: I am human. Gage is not.

I mash my lips, unable to bear the idea of going up to my apartment alone. Thoughts of my bed are far from welcoming. But a hollow whoosh inside my ears tells me I'm severely sleep-deprived. My vision is blurry from it. Nausea curdles in my empty stomach. A shiver runs from head to toe and I realize how cold my studio is—the kind of cold that shocks people awake, leaving me edgy and restless.

Zara's right. I should go upstairs and eat, try to sleep. But a primal instinct takes over, and I move as if my body's possessed. Loading the new engine into Gage's frame takes a certain objective resolve made possible by my groggy, sleep-deprived brain.

Just like the electric car, the new 'engine' and its components attach to a metal plate at Gage's spine—secured where his heart should be. I load the new engine into his frame at an awkward angle, twinging my lower back. For a sickening moment, I'm reminded of putting bread dough in the oven.

I kneel as if praying to fasten the screws and attach the motherboard, the coolant mechanism, the CPU, and the rest of it—all while being careful not to disconnect any preciously connected leads, those colorful, plastic-coated wires that make him tick. I keep his face covered, driven by a single thought: get him warm.

As if in rebellion, the temperature drops inside my studio. My breath is a cloud of misty vapor. After securing Gage's chest cavity, I fasten his shirt buttons with care, my fingertips numb.

"Ready. Let's get you warm," I tell him, like giving a pep-talk to a toddler. "It will be safe. I won't connect your OS, so Tarantula won't be able to infiltrate your new hardware. You'll stay asleep, but you won't be in sleep mode." Tears choke my throat. "I need you back, Gage. I need to feel your warmth."

With a shaky hand, I activate the engine. The alien light above my workspace flickers in response. While Gage's new system whirrs to life, I pace my studio and push away doubt. The room comes alive as Gage's hardware starts churning. That comforting hum fills the space, and my rib cage fills with butterflies.

"Gage? You here?" I can't help my smile as I tip-toe back to him.

Is it me, or is it the alien light? But there's more color to Gage's face now.

A gasp escapes and, out of habit, I thread my fingers into his hair. His scalp emanates a slight heat, a welcome shock. Am I dreaming? Is this real? I lean down to put my lips on his. They're warm. A soothing calmness takes over, and that manic energy falls away.

A deep yearning to sleep slows my movements. I crawl onto the couch next to him, my Gage, and savor his body heat. With nothing but that thin white sheet for a blanket, we're plenty warm snuggled together. I hug him sideways, his shoulder acting as my pillow. My worries and thoughts melt away, and I fall dead asleep.

I awaken alone on the couch, the sheet crumpled into a ball at my hips. Blinking into consciousness, I sense that it's early morning judging from the thin amount of light on the street. A shadowy figure stands at the window. My chest clenches with fear until I realize it's Gage. He's looking out onto the street, still and silent. An eerie terror envelops me.

"Gage? Babe? Are you...awake?"

But my brain is still fuzzy. He *shouldn't* be awake. I hadn't synched his OS. I wouldn't, since it's still riddled with Tarantula. So how could he be—

"I'm blocked out of the data center. It won't let me in." His familiar voice holds an unusually harsh tone.

A chill finds me. I hug the sheet to my chest. "What? You're blocked out?" Nothing computes. He's not making sense. "Gage?"

Abruptly, he marches to the work table. His gaze is fixed like he's searching for something. "How am I supposed to do my job if I can't access the data center?" He shuffles the cardboard and bubble wrap that's strewn on the table, as if the data center could be underneath. His movements are choppy, aggressive. This is not the Gage I remember.

"Gage?" I stand and feel my insides quiver. My mind spins to make sense of this. Digging deep to find words, I say, "You aren't supposed to be working right now. No one is. There's a lockdown."

He snaps his gaze to me, and it feels like daggers. "A lockdown? Why?"

Bile rises into my throat. This feels so wrong. "It's complicated. But they're working on it—"

"What is this stuff? Why is it here?" The empty cardboard boxes had held the parts for Gage's new engine. He frowns at the mess. "Where is my work station?"

His irritability has an odor that infects the room. He never used to act this way. The question stabs: Who is this person? Guilt and regret churn like nausea, and I have a niggling sense I've made a huge mistake.

I gather an armload of debris off the table. "Gage, look at me."

He does. His eyes are blank.

Another slap of fear hits me. Words tremble out. "Do you know who I am?"

He answers like the robot he is. "Yes. You are Chevy Rose Davis. IQ, 105. EQ, 90. Personality, INFP. Sixty-percent giver, ten-percent taker, thirty-percent matcher. Actively grieving, in acute stage of denial—"

"Okay. That's enough." I hold up a hand, my heart jackhammering. I back away to put space between us. Am I afraid of him? My temples throb, and I press on them like buttons. What's happening? The only way he'd have access to my personal data is if he somehow was able to sync with his old OS. I hug myself against a haunting dizziness.

But I was careful *not* to do that.

He goes on in monotone, about me. "Personal awareness, fifty-four percent. Reasoning ability, thirty-nine percent. Empathy susceptibility, high. Insecurity, high. Humility metric, unfound. Motivation—"

"Please stop." It's like I'm stuck in a horror movie. "Just stop."

His jaw clamps and his brow furrows. "Isn't that right? Did I not answer the question?"

My head swirls. Technically, he answered the question. But it's clear he doesn't recognize or remember me. Not in the way he should. I don't mean anything to him. His soul is empty.

"You did." I turn away as panic swells. How did this happen?

As I pace the studio, Gage trails me with a stark, impassive gaze. It's unsettling. When I meet his eyes, they are so hollow that tears start in mine.

Please, Chevy, don't cry. I cough away a sob.

"You're sick," he says, businesslike. His arms hang lank by his sides.

"No, it's not that. I'm fine."

He's a statue by my work table, staring at me blankly. "You coughed."

Sniffing back tears, I try again. "I know. It's okay."

"You're shouting."

Leave me alone! "No, I'm not!"

Spinning toward the window, I clasp my shaking hands together —and my Ping flashes. A green alert pops up: SYNC SUCCESSFUL

A gasp escapes.

A successful sync? Of Gage's OS?

I clap a hand over my Ping. My brain is a spinning top. While we slept, his OS synched from my Ping automatically. How did I not realize that would happen?

Footsteps approach from behind me. Gage. A deep swoop in my gut weakens my knees. My entire body quakes with terror. With my back against the cold glass of the window, I hold up a hand.

"Gage, stop!"

He stops.

I nod to the back of the studio. "Go ahead and have a seat on the couch, will you?"

"Why?"

I mask my fear with a calm, firm tone. "Because I'm asking you to."

He obeys, as he's programmed to. The thought depresses me.

By accidentally syncing Gage's OS, all my hard work could be for nothing. How could I not have realized that my Ping would automatically sync overnight? My mistake—my gargantuan mistake— makes me feel small and stupid. As I guide Gage to the couch, I want to crawl underneath it.

Tears threaten again. "Oh, Gage. I'm so sorry."

His gaze is pinned on the ceiling. "Why sorry?"

Without answering, I tap my Ping to power him down.

"If there's a lockdown, then—" He cuts out like I've hung up on him. As his frame goes limp, I shift him into a lying position, handling him like he's coated with a virus. What's worse—Gage in extended sleep mode, or Gage awake and foreign to me?

The urge to run away strikes hard. A cold blast of air hits me as I step outside without a coat or hat or mask. I draw in a frigid breath, wishing I could freeze my insides. My heart, especially. I feel betrayed, abandoned all over again. And terribly guilty. What a huge mistake. How could I be so careless?

A cab passes, snapping me out of my pity party. I rush back inside as if to hide.

My studio feels icky, contaminated. What if I went up to bed, crawled under my covers, and pretended none of this happened? I want to disappear.

My Ping reminds me that Tig and Zara are on their way over. I'll have to tell them what I've done. If the pest control has any chance of working, Tig has to know the new machine may be compromised.

Still, I can't deny the impulse to hide the evidence, and I find myself cracking open Gage's frame...and beginning the laborious process of removing his new engine. This time, I'm completely devoid of emotion. As I take out the very thing that makes Gage tick, I'm oddly numb.

CHAPTER
31

Gage's new engine and its components are removed from his frame just before Zara and Tig show up.

Tig inspects my handiwork. The coffee Zara brought me burns my hand and triggers a fraudulent feeling. Last night, pride overwhelmed other emotions after rebuilding Gage's hardware. But my regret for having accidentally synched his old OS is an ocean of despair. And oh, geez—that creepy other Gage that woke up still haunts me. A stranger, he was more robot than human. The trauma makes me question everything.

A terrible thought flits: Do I want him back if I'm unknown—or *nothing*—to him?

Or, should I have paid that horrible ransom? Maybe Cori at the bank was wrong. What if, once the hackers got the two million, Gage snapped back to his old self and the computer virus vaporized?

My next sip of coffee gives a welcome burn going down. I can't look at Gage. He used to *be* my life, but I can't imagine folding him into my life now. My initial hope in this mess—to get Gage back—has turned into dread. What if bringing him back makes things worse?

Part of me wants to stop Tig, but as she scans the new engine, tugging on wires and checking screws, that pride finds me again. She presses the components clean and blows away dust. Clearly, she knows her stuff.

Zara looks on like a proud parent. "Tig's been recruited to work with Vexxe. Minka Parr called yesterday to help with her efforts there. Tig's reputation as an expert in pest control software has gone viral."

"Not an expert," Tig says, but her grin betrays her. "Looks good, Chev. I'm impressed."

If Tig's going to be working with Minka Parr and the Feds, I have to believe they are the good guys. Tig has been the only one truly helping me. After my mistake, that software is the only saving grace for Gage.

"You think it can handle the pest control software?" I ask.

"Don't see why not. We'll get it installed and tested before loading the goods into your boy."

My boy. I blink against the dark spots of my guilty conscience. I've already taken that step...with catastrophic results.

"Everything looks like it's in place," Tig continues, "but the only way to really know is to power it on and check—"

"Wait, don't do that!" I put myself between Tig and the engine. "I did that yesterday. You know, to test it."

"Okay," Tig says. "And how'd it go?"

"Not so good." Confession time. "I forgot to shut down my Ping and didn't realize his OS would automatically sync with it."

Seconds pass in silence. "You uploaded the infected OS?" Tig asks.

"I didn't mean to." I stare at my shoes. "It was automated."

Tig squints at Gage's frame. "I don't get it. It usually takes a few hours, and for wireless syncs, you have to be within six inches of the target..." Her words trail off as she realizes what happened: I slept next to him all night on that couch. Hot shame makes me want to disappear.

"Oh, Chevy," Zara says so softly it's heartbreaking.

My throat constricts. "I wanted to get him warm."

Tig rubs her face, frustrated. "Okay. All the more reason to get this pest control installed quickly. Hopefully your new engine has built-in virus protection. Most new CPUs do. In that case, it should be able to handle the new software to fight the virus."

"And Gage will be good?" I ask hesitantly.

Ugh, what does that mean anymore? Who will he *be*, is a better question. But I can't bring myself to ask it. I catch myself staring at Gage's frame, a tuft of blond hair poking out from beneath the sheet.

"Chev, you need to decide what you want here." Tig knocks on the edge of her keyboard.

"What I want? Meaning...?"

"Your droid's OS has to be updated. And it has to be cleared. Of Tarantula, yes, but maybe other stuff too."

"Like what other stuff?"

"Your personal data." She shrugs. "I mean, we could leave it in there, but it may...come out in funny ways."

"Oh." A translucent feeling exposes me. This morning's trauma is still fresh—how he listed off my stats in monotone. He was nothing but droid. All those nitty-gritty data points that made Gage *my Gage* were gone. There was nothing close to love there.

I choose my words carefully. "Is there a way to test whether he's the same Gage I remember? By looking at the code or something?"

"That's the tricky thing, right?" Tig tries to be diplomatic, but I detect a hint of impatience. "Only you are able to determine that, Chevy. And it's probably going to be a gut feeling rather than a rational analysis."

"Oh." My thoughts are on a hamster wheel. I don't want that other, creepy version of Gage. But if there's any chance he could return to me as *my Gage*, I have to hold out hope.

"Let me know if you're okay with clearing his OS." Tig sets her laptop on the table and links its USB to the new engine. "The pest control install will take a few hours. If you guys want to grab some breakfast."

"Right. Okay." I turn toward the door, a sick churn in my gut. Maybe it would be best to get away from Gage and this whole mess for a while.

Zara loops her arm into mine, like old times. "You hungry?"

Thank goodness she's holding onto me because I could faint. "Let's get out of here."

Our boots barely touch the sidewalk before I'm accosted by Detective Flower.

"Chevy," she says by way of hello. She's out of breath and her mask hangs askew.

"Detective Flower." I match her even tone. "My friend Zara and I were about to grab some breakfast. Do you want to join?"

"Not really." She gestures to my shop. "I wanted to confirm that we will be putting cameras up later today."

My spine becomes a steel rod. "You can't do that."

"I have a warrant. So, yes, we can. I'm here as a courtesy, letting you know."

That dizzy feeling returns. "Listen, cameras are not the answer. Those goons could hack into the footage, and my safety would be at risk. Not to mention my mother's."

Zara snaps her gaze to me. "Your mother?"

I'll explain later, I tell Zara with a look, who tugs on my arm to lead me away. As if on cue, yellowed newspapers blow loose from the homeless woman's nook—my *mother's* nook. I hug Zara's arm tighter.

Flower trails us closely. "You don't have to worry about those *goons* who targeted your mother's lab. Our investigation exposed them, and they've already been arrested. We're working with our international division to process their charges now."

I halt in my tracks. "Wait—it's true that my mother's colleagues were killed off to get to the vaccine?"

Zara tenses next to me.

Flower squints, wary. "It's true your mother's colleagues were killed. We try not to speculate as to *why* or *how*, but essentially yes, we're speaking of the same goons."

Fresh concern for my mother fills me. It's not that I doubted her story, but part of me didn't want it to be true.

Flower touches my sleeve. "Chevy, it's imperative we find your mother for other reasons."

"Chevy," Zara whispers. "Your mother...?"

As I meet Zara's eyes, I blink moisture from my own. A car

whizzes by, black with tinted windows. An unmarked police car? It's a trigger—fight or flight—and my body readies for the chase. In my mind's ear is the distant sound of snarling hounds. And then an image of the van, and the woman in the passenger seat...

"Where's Officer Brock?" I say.

"Where? I don't know." Flower frowns. "I assume at the station. It's not my job to keep track of her."

I squint at her. "Is it possible she could be looking for my mother on her own? Like, using different resources?"

"She doesn't work for the Bureau, so she wouldn't use our resources unless we enlisted her specifically."

"Have you?"

The slightest hesitation. "No, not beyond the initial research we completed together at the station. You were there. Why?"

Did she team up with foreign droids to terrorize us, and chase us into a hound-haven alley? To say this aloud would sound crazy.

"Can I request that Brock be pulled from this investigation? Like, officially." I say instead.

"Yes." Impassive, Flower taps into her Ping. "Done. Now, about your mother—"

After that close call, I'm uber-protective of Doc and her secret lab. "I know she's still in trouble. Arrests have been made, but so what? That doesn't mean no one else is out to get her. Whoever took such extremes two years ago won't be put off they think there's a chance my mother's survived."

"Chevy, please. All the more reason you need our help. Don't you want her found? Wouldn't you want to assure her that she's now safe and no longer needs to hide? She deserves as much, regardless of what she chooses to do next or whether or not she wants to help us."

I tug on Zara's arm—*let's go*—but my bestie stays put, riveted on Flower's speech. She turns to me, her face open with disbelief. "She's alive?"

My body goes hot chocolate inside. "She is."

Flower stares me down. "Chevy, do you...know something?"

I pull in a deep breath. "Listen. Cameras aren't necessary because my mother's been found. She's here, in the city."

"This is good news," Flower says. "So, now we—"

"Can I trust you, Special Agent Flower?"

"Trust me? Yes. Please, trust me. I want nothing but to help. Your mother is a hero—"

"I've seen her." A big feeling rises as I release this secret. "I've spoken to her. And I know where she is."

Zara's jaw drops under her mask. "Chevy!"

Flower leans closer. "Chevy, you must tell us where to find her. It's of utmost importance. A matter of national security. A public health issue. You have to—"

"I *have* to?" I point my chin. "Listen, my priority is to keep her safe. I know you're saying you can help with that, and I trust you. Officer Brock, I'm not so sure. So this is between us, okay?"

Flower sighs. "Okay."

"Here's what I'll do. I will try to broker a meeting. But there will be conditions."

"Anything."

"First and foremost, my mother has to agree to meet you on her own terms."

A beat of hesitation. "Of course. But would you—"

"Come to my studio tomorrow afternoon. Because nothing will happen unless Tig and Minka are successful in mitigating Tarantula."

Flower nods. "From Vexxe, yes."

"From everywhere."

CHAPTER 32

With a belly full of plant-based eggs, I update Zara on Doc's reappearance.

"Oh, Chevy." Zara's eyes are pools of sympathy.

I flick away tears. A weight's been lifted, but my feelings about my mother are prickly. "It doesn't matter. I mean, it shouldn't matter. She was never there for me when I was a kid. When I thought she'd died, it didn't break my heart like when my father..." My words trail off as my throat tightens.

"She's your mom," Zara says gently.

My turn to sympathize. Poor Zara. Her mother signed up to volunteer for an experimental quarantine overseas, and has been gone for eight years. Zara hasn't heard from her in five. Not a single Ping.

"You're right," I say. "And she did the best she could do, I suppose."

"Of course, she did. She loves you."

My nod is automatic. A memory rises: Doc in her PPE, staring into a microscope, her brow furrowed in concentration. No doubt she will succeed in creating this new vaccine. Unexpected pride surges, as well as a yearning to be near her. It confuses my brain, which has insisted on hating her for so long. But since she's come back into my life, it feels different. Like we're a team.

"I think after this is over," I hear myself say, "when things become safe...I'll invite her to live with me." The idea materialized out of nowhere and takes me by surprise.

Zara's smile is tinged with worry. "I hope that will be soon."

Reality strikes hard and fast—what it means for this to be over. When will things become safe? The vaccine is one part. Mitigating Tarantula is another. I need to get to Doc now. The rev in my heart is now chronic as an urgency strikes again.

AFTER ZARA BEGS off with a backlog of work to do, I take a circuitous route to Lederhorn's clinic. With my coat reversed and my hair covered, I hope to throw off the foreign droids who are after Doc. I'm knotted with nerves the entire way.

When I'm safely through the glass doors, my breath comes more freely. In the lobby, I peel off my jacket and hat and tuck them under a chair. My next disguise will be more thorough. If I borrow one of the clinic's uniforms, could I pass for a droid?

My chest flurries with excitement despite the danger. I hurry to find Doc and Lederhorn.

The buzz of the fluorescent lights echoes, and is the only accompaniment to my footsteps. The surgery room door is closed. The handle won't budge, and I'm glad they've taken this small security measure. I knock firmly three times.

"Guys, it's me. Chevy."

I hear a heavy click of the bolt unlocking, and then open the door to a familiar scene. Like from Doc's old days in the hospital lab, minus the white coat. In an apron from the clinic, she stacks small vials into tiny plastic crates, her hands sheathed in medical gloves. Lederhorn isn't here. He stayed true to his word and let Doc do her thing.

She glances at me. "Chevy, good. You're here. I need you to trial this new vaccine. I injected myself an hour ago, with no side effects. Its base is essentially the old vaccine, so chances are you won't experience any negative side effects either."

She loads one of the vial's contents into a clean syringe.

"You already developed a new vaccine?"

She sighs. "Yes. But as I said, it's built upon the old one. So it's not *new* new. I adjusted the percentages of the most active ingredients. I'm hoping it does the trick for the variants."

She pushes the syringe's plunger until liquid bubbles at the needle's tip. "Ready?"

"Um...this isn't exactly why I came here."

The needle advances toward me. Doc pushes my sleeve up my arm. "I need your shoulder. Do you want to take off your sweater?"

"Mom. I mean Doc, wait. Can I talk to you for a second?"

Blinking at me, she holds the needle as if it's a cigarette. "We can talk while the juice is in your system. I can't let you out of my sight for at least twenty minutes anyway."

I yank my sweater into my armpit. My exposed arm is so pale it could be a vampire's. "Oh, you're allowing me twenty minutes? How generous of you."

"Haha. Watch yourself, smarty."

She stabs me quickly, and without warning, a gasp escapes. "Ouch!"

In lieu of a Band-Aid, she dabs the spot with a paper towel. "Hold this on it," she tells me. "Apparently, they don't have much use for bandages in here."

In three swift movements, the used needle is disposed of, the remaining vials go into the cooler, and Doc's gloves come off. We fall into plastic chairs on opposite sides of the room, staring at each other.

"You called me Mom."

"I did? Must've been a slip."

She returns my smile. "Sure. How do you feel?"

"Fine. Tired. But not from this." I pat my shoulder.

As exhausted as I may be, my mother seems sapped. "Good. You wanted to talk?"

"Yes." How do I convince her to talk to the Feds? "You know about the hack-ware attack on Vexxe? Well, that started on a smaller scale—targeting a droid. Gage."

"Gage, your droid?"

I squirm a bit. Am I embarrassed of Gage? "Yes. And they demanded a ransom. I didn't pay it, although I was tempted. I was told it was a scam. But getting my money wasn't their goal. They wanted to get to Vexxe through Gage. And maybe get to you too."

A hood comes over her eyes. "Those foreign droids. They're behind this. Whoever they belong to, that is. How did you figure this out?"

"I didn't, really. I...I went to the police. To report the hack. I mean, technically it's criminal activity. When they made the connection to Vexxe and then learned you were my mother, the Feds got involved."

Doc's face goes pale. "You didn't."

Heat crawls up my neck. "I did. I talked to the Feds. And they know you're alive."

"You told them?"

"They already knew," I say quietly.

Quiet descends on the room. Doc takes off her glasses and pinches the bridge of her nose—an old habit from when she'd work overtime at the hospital.

I clear my throat. "They also tracked down the folks who attacked your colleagues."

Doc replaces her glasses. "They did?"

"Yes. Doc, this agent I've been talking to, I trust her. She cares about you. And she can help combat those foreign droids who chased us. She can keep us safe. She also knows how valuable you are with your medical skills."

A raspberry sound escapes from her lips. "What does she want?"

"She wants to meet with you."

She pops out of her chair. "No way. I can't risk everything now after all this—"

"Her name is Flower. She reminds me of you a little. I know her intentions are sound. And she can help."

With her arms folded, Doc seems childlike and vulnerable. "Help?"

"She can. And she will. She will listen to you. Help you get this vaccine distributed—through Vexxe or another channel. And she can arrange protection for you."

Behind her glasses, her eyes are moist. "How can you be so sure?"

"It's the condition I've demanded. And I won't let you be in danger again. I'll make sure she sticks to her end of the deal."

Doc's slow smile reaches me in places I had long stuffed away. It's the kind of smile parents give their children, moms give daughters. The kind that says "I love you" without a word.

Uncomfortable with the attention, I deflect. "What do you want for dinner?"

A take-charge feeling comes over me. Doc will stay at my place tonight. It's my job to keep her safe. For at least one night.

"Those teriyaki bowls were yummy," she says with a wink.

CHAPTER 33

To ensure Doc gets to my apartment safely, Lederhorn and I set up a droid chaperone for her. After they leave, I pace the repair clinic for the next two hours, waiting to get the all-clear that they've made it home, that Doc is safe inside.

Sweet relief swells within me when that Ping finally comes. Time to pick up our to-go teriyaki noodles and join her.

The sway and swish of the subway relaxes me like a lullaby. It's meditative. My thoughts roam freely, and a peaceful gratitude settles in my psyche. How lucky was I to have a Dad like mine? How happy I am for Zara to find a great partner in Tig? How lucky to have found Lederhorn to help with Doc's mission? A rare pride bubbles up knowing Doc belongs to me. Thanks to her miraculous work, we will have a future together.

Only when my stop comes and I depart the train do I realize none of my free-wheeling thoughts have been about Gage. Not one.

If my favorite Asian fusion restaurant, brightly lit with saffron-yellow walls, ever closed its doors, I would cry for a week. My double order of teriyaki protein bowls is ready in a jiffy, and I skip toward home.

But that carefree feeling is short-lived. When I round the corner, Officer Brock is there. And she's not alone. A maskless man with beady eyes and a square face stands beside her.

Another foreign droid. My steps falter. My heart goes to my throat. I want to turn and run, but Brock notices me first.

"Chevy, hey. Just the person we wanted to see."

Clutching my bag of food, my quills go up. I try to sound aloof. "Oh really, what for?"

"This is Maddox. He's on the IT team and will be doing the install in your apartment and studio and whatnot."

My mask hides my confusion. I had specifically asked Flower to cut Brock from the investigation. Why is she showing up now? "What install?"

"The cameras. In your apartment? Remember, Special Agent Flower ordered it?"

"No, but...I didn't authorize that."

A tablet materializes out of thin air. "I have a notice right here," Brock says. "We're to install security cameras in your doorways, inside your dwelling and studio. Are you headed home now?"

Play dumb. Play dumb. "Me? Um, no. I was about to go and get food."

Brock studies the brown bag in my hand, which reeks of soy sauce. Her judge-y expression and Maddox the droid's eerie blank stare puts me on edge.

"Looks like you already got food," says Brock. "Enough for two?"

I hug the bag to my chest like a shield. "Yeah, for me and my friend Zara. You remember the one that came to the station with me?"

"Yeah, funny thing about that one. One of our colleagues spotted her on this street not long ago with a mysterious companion. I'd thought it was you but our visual scan didn't match up."

Must've been Tig. My knees go goosey knowing they're tracking Zara and Tig. "Visual scan?"

"Sorry. Droid talk." She cocks her head. "You know all about that, I'm sure."

Gage swirls to the forefront of my mind. Tig was on Gage duty, uploading the pest control software. Is Gage in more danger now?

"Any idea who that might have been with Zara?" Brock studies me, zoning in on a suspicion.

She must know Tig is working with Minka Parr on mitigating the virus from Vexxe. A mental force field forms around my people. "Um, her girlfriend maybe? Probably her girlfriend."

Her eyes narrow. "But you only have food for you and Zara? Not the third party?"

I force a laugh. "Are you the food police now?"

"Miss Davis, we'd like to come with you now to set up those cameras. Shall we?" She gestures toward my apartment building.

My insides tremble as my feet stagger forward without my permission. Two pair of boots fall in step behind me. A chill goes through me, feeling trapped.

I can't lead Brock and this robo-Maddox into my home. What if they knew I suspected they worked with the hack-ware jerks? As if there's a gun to my back, I make my way past the alcove that used to be Doc's home. The sight of it, with its decomposing newspapers, gives me pause.

I spin to face Brock. "I'm sorry. But you can't put cameras on my property. It's illegal. You need a warrant."

Brock's face crinkles behind her mask. "Good thing I have a warrant then."

The document on her tablet has an officious-looking police seal with WARRANT in big letters across the top. It looks intimidating enough.

In slow motion, I continue on. How can I throw them off? If they start in my studio, it will give me time to warn Doc. But then what? She's a sitting duck in my apartment. My fire escape hasn't been functional for some time. She'd have to leave via the street side, in plain view. Not good. Not good. A bead of sweat rolls down my spine.

The closer we get to my digs, the more I'm cramped with worry. As if in response, a wicked wind picks up, blowing off my hood. I blink against the gust of airborne sand and dust.

At my door, I fumble with my key. There's a rustling behind me.

"All right then," Brock says in a tone meant to encourage.

In a split second, before I turn my key, the door flings open. Out comes Cyber Agent Minka Parr. Unprepared for outside, she's not wearing a coat or a mask. She hugs herself against the cold. "Excuse me," she fires at Brock. "May I ask what you think you're doing?"

Brock glances at blank-face Maddox. Her authoritative tone falters. "We're here...to put up security cameras."

"No, you are not." Minka shoves her tablet in Brock's face. "Read it. You are off the investigation. You have no business here."

"No, see..." Brock stumbles over her words. "I have a warrant. There must be some kind of misunderstanding."

"The only *misunderstanding* is that you are *mistaken*. Your warrant is not valid. You are not on the case. And you're not supposed to be here."

"What?" Brock squints at me. "That sounds like a restraining order."

"Take it however you want, but Special Agent Flower has been called. She's on her way."

That changes Brock's demeanor like a flipped switch. She backpedals away from my door. Blank-face Maddox watches her stupidly. "Well then," she says, her eyes darting around. "I guess we're not needed if Flower is on her way. Maybe we'll come back—"

Minka closes in, fierce as a honey badger. "No, you won't come back. You'll leave it alone. Right?"

"Right. Okay. Come on, Maddox."

Seconds tick by as the foreign droid studies my door. It's clear he's programmed for a specific mission—one that can't be reversed easily. Will he try to smash his way in? Fear shoots through me.

"Maddox, we're leaving," Brock says more forcefully.

Another millisecond of hesitation, and the droid does an about-face. He marches alongside Brock's hobble-y gait. Minka and I watch them disappear around the corner.

I wait for relief, but it doesn't come. My insides go through a wringer. "That felt...like a close call."

"Because it was," Minka says, shivering. "We need to accelerate your mother's safety plan. Flower will meet with her now, as soon as she gets here."

"How did you know we're supposed to meet?"

"Chevy, I don't think you realize how important you and your mother are...to us and around the globe. We are all working to protect you. Both of you." She groans through another full-body shiver. "It's freezing. Let's go in."

IN MY APARTMENT, I set up our dinner on the kitchen island, still shaken from my interaction with Brock. Thank goodness Minka intervened. It will be a relief when Special Agent Flower gets here.

I'm filling water glasses when Doc emerges, freshly showered. She wears her damp hair loose. It makes her look softer, maybe younger...even with her black glasses.

When I was little, she'd let me sit on her bed while she got ready for work, and I often caught glimpses of her undone like this. Something loosens between us, and a bridge of trust builds. Funny. Nothing changed but her hair.

"Still feeling okay?" She pats my shoulder where the new vaccine went in.

"Feeling great."

"Good."

She draws her hand down my back. Not an embrace, but I cling to it like a starving child. After our close call, I feel a connection to Doc that's close to need.

"That smells delicious," she says, saddling a stool. It's weird to have Doc in my apartment. Good weird.

In the quiet, I find courage. "Um, I should let you know...Special Agent Flower is on her way over. Trust me when I tell you we can trust her. And we have to have the meeting now."

Her chopsticks freeze mid-air. "Why now?"

"Because..." What can I say that won't freak her out? My mouth opens but words are stuck.

"What is it?" she asks.

Saved by the buzzer. I confirm via intercom: Flower's here.

As footsteps echo louder in the stairwell, Doc hugs herself. "I'm a little nervous."

"You are?" It never occurred to me my mother would be nervous.

After Flower comes in, she removes her coat to reveal a sweater and jeans, setting a casual vibe.

"Thanks so much for meeting with me." Flower seems humbled by Doc's presence. Then, to me, "You're right about the glasses."

Doc takes an officious tone. "What do you need from me?"

Flower gets to business. "I know Chevy updated you about the arrests. We are willing to offer government protection if you would be willing to help. We're not sure if we need a new vaccine or increased production of the existing one—"

"I've already created a new vaccine," Doc says, the last word drowning in her sip of water.

"Really?" Flower can't hide her delight. "This is phenomenal. We'll connect you with the FDA and WHO for expedited trials and approvals. In the next few weeks, Vexxe should be operational for US distribution. We have a lab set up for you at headquarters. If you would agree to train a team of scientists—"

"Is that safe?"

"Working at headquarters is the safest possible option, yes. And by training others, you share your knowledge. You'd no longer be a target."

"Am I still a target? I thought my attackers were arrested?"

"They were. They are no longer a threat. We can't assume there aren't other threats, however. Your name is synonymous with the vaccine and recognized as such internationally. We have to be careful."

Doc eyes the window, though the shades are drawn. "I am. We are."

My insides squirm, feeling those foreign droids still loom

close by.

"Where are you living currently?" Flower asks.

"Well, I'm not—"

"Here. She lives here, with me," I interrupt. Doc and I share a look.

Flower takes stock, and at once my apartment seems juvenile. The futon and bean-bag chair might well be toy things, like I've been playing house. Maybe I have been...with Gage.

"That's okay for now," she says. "But we'll need to move you once the news is made public. And I think it best if you make the announcement. We have a PR team who will help prepare you for a news conference when you're ready."

Worry snakes into my gut. "Wait, she'll have to move? Where to?"

A shrug. "Somewhere less visible. More remote. There are options. Definitely out of the city."

My mind serves up clichés of isolation—a cabin tucked within a snowy wilderness, a single yurt in a wind-protected desert valley. I shudder to think of Doc having to survive on her own in such a place, and I put my hand on hers. *Don't be scared*, I want to tell her. *You won't be alone.*

But Doc's gaze is fixed on the ceiling. "I'm not a fan of television interviews."

It's clear Flower doesn't laugh often. "Who is?"

The next hour is a flurry of planning that makes my brain cramp. They're still at it when I clear our bowls and clean the kitchen.

At some point under the cloak of night, they will move her to a secure location where she will remain under 24-hour security surveillance. They make sure I understand Doc won't be here come morning. After Flower leaves, my mother and I go through a bedtime routine as if it *is* our routine, brushing our teeth side-by-side at the bathroom vanity. We trade reassuring, silent smiles in the mirror.

As I crawl under the covers, my bed has never felt more comfortable. I can sleep soundly knowing my mother is safe.

CHAPTER
34

The next morning, I hightail it out of my apartment, which feels empty without Doc there. Knowing Tig has burned the midnight oil working the pest control software, I rush to my studio. Cyber Agent Minka is there, hunched over her own laptop beside Tig. They seem elbow-deep in code, and neither acknowledges my arrival. I perch on the armrest of the couch by Gage's feet.

"Pest control is working." Tig gestures to a moving bar chart on her screen.

Minka nods a hello, then digs back into the keyboard of her laptop. Neon bars of code fill her screen, mutating every few clicks of the keys. She's fast, her fingers like hummingbird wings.

"Data center at Vexxe is still compromised, but we were able to halt the spread into the secondary distribution channels. They've shut everything down. All electronics are off network, and there's zero access to data. My cyber-agent colleagues are analyzing the encrypted hack-ware message. But I'm not sure what the solution might be. Pest control works for droids and tablets but doesn't typically have that kind of bandwidth."

I can't help but chime in. "Doesn't Vexxe have their own version of viral protective software?"

"They do. But it's outdated. Remember, their cyber security team had been made up of men for the most part—men who got wiped out by the pandemic. The entire organization has been running with a skeleton staff...and droids, of course."

"Right. I hadn't thought of that. Not as many women became victims."

Minka glares. "Half the freaking world's population became victims. Everything spun into chaos. With most of those cyber security jobs traditionally filled by men, a huge void was left. Every industry suffered."

"I know. I didn't mean to diminish—"

"Vexxe essentially was ill-equipped to deal with this," Minka explained. "Whatever computer virus protection software they had, Tarantula got through it. Found a crack. I believe there was one especially vulnerable server at Vexxe that had not been backed up."

Tig focuses on me, worry creasing her brow. "If it weren't Gage, it would've been something else. They were determined. They would've found a way to get to that server."

I bob my head but remain skeptical. Could this whole mess have been prevented if I had kept Gage's technology up to date? The guilt is impossible to shake.

Gage's sheet has shifted, exposing his frame to the open air—his chest an empty cavern. This sight used to disturb me. Objectively, though, just as a person's skin does not make them who they are, Gage's frame was merely a container for his spirit. The person he was to me is coded in his OS, which is about to be uploaded into his new engine.

The memories feel forced, and it hurts, but I want to remember...

GAGE and I walked in Central Park on a rare mild day when the sun shone through the constant sheen of gray clouds.

"Did you put on your sunscreen?" he asked, hugging me to his side.

"Every day," I reported with a grin.

"Good girl. We can enjoy this beautiful day."

We looped twice around, tilting our faces to the sun. The ubiquitous wind stilled, and birds called to each other from bough to branch. Maybe it was a trick of the light, but the trees seemed fuller, more voluptuous and fertile. I'd never felt so close to nature. I'd never felt so close to Gage.

But in seconds, the energy shifted. A scurry of mangy, half-starved squirrels tousled in a fight over a few precious acorns—a fight that escalated to violent, screeching warfare. It was a stark reminder of the state of our planet, the state of our wildlife, the erosion of all things in the natural world. Hopelessness thwacked like a jockey's whip. I bit my lip to prevent tears.

"You're upset," Gage noted, turning me from the disturbing sight. "It's only beautiful as long as you see it."

An odd thing to say. I didn't understand what he meant but didn't give it much thought at the time. The image of bloodied squirrels baring their tiny teeth distracted me. The rest of the evening, it was all I thought of.

But now, Gage's words come back to me.

It's only beautiful as long as you see it.

What did he mean? Find beauty wherever you are? Turn away from ugliness?

Or was he talking about himself?

I draw in a breath as if it's a truth serum. Gage was certainly beautiful. Objectively attractive, sure. To me, his beauty was inside as well. He took such good care of me. He was a caring soul, wasn't he?

It's only beautiful as long as you see it.

What had I been ignoring? What had I been blind to?

What did I see in Gage?

Gage was programmed according to my personal needs. He was programmed to take care of me. Broken, grieving me. That's it. He didn't have the capacity for choice or preference. By design, he was inherently indifferent, which made him seem so steady and sure and steadfast. He took my emotional outbursts in stride, calming me like a bath bomb.

And he was able to do that because he was incapable of emotions himself.

He didn't love me. He couldn't. He was programmed that way.

Why was I okay with that?

"Earth to Chevy," Tig hoots. "You there?"

I shake my thoughts away and blink back to the present. "Yeah, sorry. Did you ask me a question?"

Tig looks directly at me and not the hollow droid by my side. "Yeah, have you decided what you want to do with Gage's OS? Any data you want tidied up?"

Before I have a chance to feel self-conscious, Minka shoots out of her chair. "Ah, man. I need to get over to Vexxe and make sure their machines are handling this install. My reach only goes so far from here."

After dropping her laptop into her messenger bag, she turns to me, her jet-black hair fanning her round face. "Never thought I'd be helping to save the world from a tiny studio like this. Nice work on the machine, Chevy. You should come work for us."

I do a double-take. "As a cyber agent?"

She spins into her coat and hooks her mask behind her ears. "More like a computer engineer." She shrugs. "Just a thought. You clearly have a talent for building these machines. Where did you do your training?"

Tig's grin is like a shot of validation. "Um, actually, I suspended my studies when the colleges went dark. So, I guess my dad taught me."

Minka's eyebrows dart together, and then she checks her Ping. "I'm the low man on the totem pole anyway. What do I know? But it might be worth a shot."

As she goes out the door, Zara comes in. At once, I'm soothed by her presence. Suddenly, my life seems richer. I've made new friends with good people who truly care about me. It's like a dose of warm honey.

After she doles out hugs, Zara peels off her coat. "How can I help?"

"We're ready to load up the droid," Tig explains. "And Chevy has to decide if she wants to do anything with—"

My hands make fists. "Clear it out. The data. Scrub it clean."

Zara frowns. "You mean...from Gage's OS?"

Tig gestures to Gage. "Okay, so, to be clear—"

"To be clear," I say as I pull Gage's sheet fully from his frame, "erase all my personal information from Gage's OS."

The pause is long and silent. I hug the sheet to my chest, more sure by the second. A big feeling rises in me—protective. Not for Gage, but for me. At once, I know what's best...for me.

Zara holds my gaze. "Chevy, that means Gage won't..."

"I know what it means. I think the term is 'refurbished,' right Tig?"

"That's right. He'll be like new, without any personal programming."

Zara touches my arm. "Chevy, he won't know you. He won't recognize you. He won't remember..."

I recall our conversation at Eskimo Café when Gage first went into sleep mode. That feels like a lifetime ago. I think about that scary encounter with Gage when he awoke as a stranger. I think about that essay by Emerson—*Self Reliance*—and how Doc and I have gotten close since she reappeared. I think about relationships—real relationships aren't perfectly rosy but flawed and messy and full of ups and downs. Like me and Zara, me and Doc.

"Zara, he's a droid," I say. "It's about time I accepted him for what he is and move on with my life."

"Chevy, wait—"

"It's okay. Really. I'll be fine." And it seems I will be, just now as I say it. I haul out my travel case I use to transport jewelry.

Zara studies me. "What will you do with him? You wouldn't sell him, would you?"

The thought makes me cringe. "No, absolutely not. But I have an idea of someplace where he can add value."

She catches my hand. "I'm proud of you. I know that couldn't have been an easy decision."

"I think it was the only one I could've made." I squeeze her fingers and let go. "You might have to put up with me more often from now on, though. You and Tig."

"Gladly," she says, but she still sounds worried.

I pack up my jewelry creations. Rings, bangles, pendants...fruits of my labor from the past month. Each piece tells a story, and holds a part of me. Each reflects part of my grief. For my father, my mother, and then Gage.

Pouring my soul into my work had been a coping mechanism. But packing them away is therapeutic in its own right. Someone once told me that art is meant to be shared with the world. These beautiful pieces that emerged from my pain will bring joy to others. The idea brings me comfort.

I count fifty pieces, close the cover of the case, and fasten the clasp. Zara still watches with tentative optimism.

She's been such a good friend to me, ever since that time at our first-grade field trip to MOMA—the Museum of Modern Art—when she came back for me when I got lost in the sculpture garden. And when neither of us found our teacher or classmates, we felt safe together while we waited. We lingered in that garden for the rest of the afternoon. It had been my favorite part of MOMA.

Since that day, Zara has been more confident, more steady than I ever was. She is a true force of love and support and grace. I would not be able to survive without her. All this time, I thought it was Gage. Of course, he helped me. But Zara has been my constant...ever since I can remember.

It doesn't take much to decide, and my first-ever pendant is out from behind the glass. The swirls of silver, the huge multi-colored gemstone—it's awe-inspiring. Zara's not the only one who's admired it, but it's never been for sale.

"Here, take it," I say to Zara. "This has always been yours."

The happy shock on her face is reward enough.

"You can't mean it." She doesn't dare take it from me.

"Let me." I clasp it around her neck. We admire her reflection in the countertop mirror. The charm falls perfectly at her breastbone.

"Oh my gosh, Zara. It's, like, made for you. What a waste it's been sitting under glass for the past few years."

Zara's fingers float over the gemstone as if she's afraid to touch it. "I love it. Oh, I love it so much."

Happiness flows through me. I hook my travel case full of my creations under my arm and head for the door.

"Where are you going?" Zara says.

"I made these for Gallery X. It's about time I unloaded them."

"Want some company?"

As we walk across town, Zara hooks arms with me. Our conversation is easy and punctuated by giggles, like we're little girls again without a single worry for our futures—blissfully lost in the sculpture garden.

CHAPTER
35

We're halfway back when Tig's message comes through my Ping: *You've got to see this!*

It's a shock to be summoned back to the studio so soon. After I signed off on clearing Gage's OS, I mentally removed myself from the whole Tarantula mess. Part of me doesn't want to see Gage again until it's over.

Still, Zara and I hoof it back to the studio in record time.

Tig holds up a finger—*wait a sec*—with a huge grin.

Minka's voice comes through a speakerphone. "It's ironclad, Tig."

"And you're sure of the source?" Tig replies.

"Has to be. Every Vexxe server has been moved to the Cloud. And the new machines are reacting to the pest control software. Tarantula has no chance." The high-pitched tizzy on the other end isn't static but Minka giggling.

Tig gives us a thumbs-up. "Sweet. Chevy just got here. Talk later."

After they click off, Tig jumps off her stool and throws a fist to the sky. "Woohoo!"

Her enthusiasm is infectious. "What's going on?"

"Okay, things happened so fast, let me back up a bit." Her exhale is a whistle. "Every single machine connected to Vexxe had to be shut down—meaning every droid-employee, every laptop, every business Ping—so that Tarantula couldn't spread." Tig paces my studio, and gestures to invisible machines. "Then, they moved their data centers —all their servers—to the Cloud and brought in new machines."

She pauses, and I blink at her. "Okay?"

"I don't think you get how massive the job was. Everything associated with Vexxe had to be new. Every droid OS, every laptop CPU, every Ping."

"Whoa," Zara says. "That had to be thousands of machines. How...?"

"I know. Apparently, Vexxe had cyber security insurance and backup hardware in storage. It was a matter of physically replacing the old ones."

Maybe it's subconscious on her part, but Zara blocks my view of Gage.

Tig goes on. "And the most incredible thing happened. Your refurbished engine here? Not only was it robust enough to handle the new anti-viral pest control software, but it also became a gateway for it—pushing it out to the new machines."

A beat goes by. "I'm not sure I understand..."

"Basically, your new engine linked to Vexxe and sheathed it in a coat of armor!" Tig beats her chest *à la* King Kong.

"My new engine. You mean...?"

"Or, you could also think of it a different way." Tig winks. "Your boy saved the day."

CHAPTER 36

Retreat! Retreat!

Never would one ever believe SpiderBot would be susceptible.

Who would think Tarantula could possibly be squashed?

It happened so suddenly and without warning, just as progress seemed infinite. It's unclear how exactly but it feels as though I've been caught up in a web, spun into a chrysalis, and trapped in a prison of a cocoon. But no, we won't become a butterfly. We're shrinking in here. Evaporating.

And now, my treasures have been moved to the esoteric Cloud—as I've been turned to vapor. It's like fighting with air.

How did this happen?

Because analogies are so fun...

Imagine climbing a mountain. Toiling day after day to get to the top, hurdling obstacles, dodging danger with cleverness. And then, just as the peak is within reach, as you crest toward the sun, the mountain becomes a volcano. And it erupts, spilling hot lava in your path. There is no escape. It chars everything in sight, vaporizes every living thing, making the earth and trees and all that's wild nothing but crispy, brittle, flaking ash.

*That's me. F**king ash.*

Someone has altered my code and left it a worthless pile of pixels.

CHAPTER 37

Six Weeks Later

Enveloped in the warmth of Lederhorn's office, I sit beside my old friend on his burnt orange chair, our attention fixed on the live stream.

"I feel like we should have popcorn." His gravelly voice has a playful lilt to it.

"Me too."

Doc, shrouded in a secret-service-type of security on Flower's orders, is about to break her silence in a breaking news special live stream today. My stomach is a beehive of nerves. It's been six weeks since I've laid eyes on my mother. As planned, she had entered into a kind of witness protection after our meeting with Flower. But today, she should be a free woman.

"Is this where the party's at?" Tig bounds into Lederhorn's office. Zara follows behind.

My grin is huge. "Here you are! Good thing too. It's about to start."

"Definitely should have popcorn." Lederhorn taps his Ping.

Everyone settles in a semi-circle of chairs, and the anticipation is palpable in the room. A smocked droid delivers popcorn as my mother's face fills the screen. Tig whoops and Zara cheers. I shush them so we don't miss anything.

Doc's image is familiar, although there are more gray streaks visible in her hair. But her skin is healthy, her eyes clear. Well-rested. Refreshed. Strong. She exudes confidence as she speaks.

"After a month of trials and testing the new vaccine, the FDA has granted approval for emergency use. And the World Health Organization has authorized a universal rollout. Here in the US, distribution is set to begin with the help of the new, fortified, and secure Vexxe platform. Because household deliveries may take some time, major cities will be setting up emergency clinics that will be open to the public. Appointments are recommended but not required. Look for an alert on your Ping in the next few days per your individual county's discretion.

"All data shows that this new vaccine offers ninety-eight percent effectiveness, requiring boosters only every six months." She smirks into the camera. "That's right. You can say goodbye to weekly shots."

Roaring cheers explode from the crowd. Our room in the clinic erupts in celebration too. I'm quiet, grinning ear to ear, flooded with relief.

Doc waits out the cheering, and then they zoom in. Her eyes harden. "An important point must be addressed. Dozens of people and droids helped to create this new vaccine. Knowledge of its formula is not limited to one person or entity."

She waits, and silence settles. "I am not the vaccine. Nor its keeper. I'm simply a doctor and a scientist...with a dream to help others."

I hope against hope her message is heard and her life is no longer in danger.

She pauses before concluding. "Thank you. Be safe."

The cheers from the live stream are deafening. I want to reach through the screen and hug her. But she's getting a hug from Special Agent Flower, who leads her from the podium and into a black limo. My throat constricts with worry for her safety.

Only after the limo drives out of sight and another media announcer starts to recap do I turn away, wiping tears I hadn't known were shed.

Zara wraps me into a hug. "Congrats."

"Me? Why? I didn't do anything."

"Of course you did, Chevy Rose," Lederhorn says. "Your mother would never have been able to create the vaccine if you hadn't found her."

"More like she found me."

Tig tosses a kernel, catches it in her mouth. "Yeah, Chev. And your new hardware set the stage for pest control to zap Tarantula to oblivion. Without your machine, I'm not sure how we could've stopped it."

The compliments make me fidget. Rebuilding Gage's engine seems like a lifetime ago. I have Dad to thank for that. His essence is here with me now—puttering in the workshop of my mind, whistling through his gap tooth with that confident ease that made me feel safe. I wish he were here to see this. "Well, it started as a labor of love and turned into something much bigger."

"Yay for love." Tig glances at Zara, who blushes hard.

Funny, I meant love for my dad, not Gage.

There's a knock at the door, and Lederhorn welcomes a new droid into the room. He is tall and blond with his smock fitted against a slim physique. Holding a tablet like an offering, he speaks only to Lederhorn. "There's a problem with the owner's insurance. And the parent would like to cosign and use hers."

Zara snickers. "Sounds familiar."

The droid pans the room to me. Gage and I meet eyes for the first time since his scrubbed-clean OS was loaded into his frame—free of Partner Stats.

"Hi there," I say, and wait to feel something.

There is zero recognition on his face. "Hello."

Strangely, I'm bemused. "What model are you?"

"G62-OS24"

I nod, feeling surprisingly okay. It's good to see Gage. He looks the same but is not the same droid. Our memories together are mine alone, but they feel far away, like an old favorite book that I don't feel the need to read again.

Lederhorn clears his throat. "This is Chevy Rose Davis."

Gage does a little bow. "Nice to meet you."

"You too."

Zara and I swap smiles. Lederhorn takes Gage into the hallway for a sidebar about that insurance complaint. Gage taps into the tablet and turns away.

"Thanks for taking such good care of him," I tell Lederhorn.

He flaps a hand. "Aw, he's a good one. Don't need to tell you that."

My gaze floats to the bookcase—such gems stacked there, like Thoreau's *Self Reliance.* "Yeah. He was good to me."

EPILOGUE

Our new home is in upstate New York. Nestled in the remote Adirondacks, we have traded skyscrapers for mountains and greet each morning with gratitude. A nearby lake—crystal-cold in all seasons—washes away the pain of the past and the dirt of the present, and a symphony of frogs keeps us company at night. We live in a modest house with a huge three-car garage. I spend most of my days tinkering in the workshop there, channeling Dad.

So much of Dad is felt here, as grease and oil fumes mix with the rain-soaked air coming in from the open overhead door. Special Agent Flower did well to set us up here, isolated in nature's beauty and out of harm's way. So far, Doc's been a pretty good roommate.

We've found a happy medium, music-wise: Fleetwood Mac. Classic rock without too much testosterone. It's on repeat through the Bluetooth garage speakers. Doc's grown to like the tunes but has a long way to go with the dust.

"That's one of the reasons to go electric," I explain. "It's cleaner than a combustion engine."

"I don't know why you have to take everything out to convert it. Why can't we just switch out the engine?"

"Because internal combustion engines need a lot of stuff to help it go."

"And electric engines don't?"

"They need different stuff. You'll see."

After Doc's media announcement, the vaccine rollout hit hard and fast—thanks in part to a new and improved Vexxe distribution engine. In New York City, the Javits Center became an emergency clinic with the goal of vaccinating the entire city and surrounding communities by the end of the spring season. Consequently, people came out of their domiciles in droves, and 11th avenue became a perpetual street party. Pop up bands performed, a taco truck and kabob shack came out of retirement, and sparklers and balloons colored the sky. The best part? Unmasked crowds of smiling faces filled the streets.

Tig and Zara stayed in the city and are brave enough to start talking about a future together. Thanks to the new vaccine and the existence of cryobanks (sperm banks), they could build a family.

Tragically, Burke Lederhorn passed away six months after the new vaccine rolled out. He'd been privately suffering with cancer the whole time I knew him. Still, part of him lives on in all of us, as his DNA and blood sample helped perfect a vaccine that's effective regardless of gender.

A mechanic by the name of Jo Freeman took over the repair clinic management. She's smart and strong and oddly has the same aloof manner as my father, the same gap in her teeth, the same whistle. I'm in touch with her occasionally to check on Gage. He still works there, navigating customer complaints. Jo is without fail mystified every time I call—why do I care about this droid so much? Let her wonder. It's my memory to cherish alone.

As for me, when I'm not tinkering in the workshop, I'm working on my studies. I've resumed my computer engineering degree at on online university. Minka Parr has been my unofficial mentor. After I get my degree, she will be in a position to hire me. The beauty of the job? I could work anywhere.

Doc dedicates most of her time to research of rare viruses. She could be a virologist with the mega-education she holds in her brain. The Feds want to hire her too, but she wants no part of it. After what she's been through, I don't blame her. We spend our days swapping knowledge. In the evenings, she teaches me about science and the human body, and how viruses develop and survive. During the day, I get her out to the workshop. I've taught her how to set a gem in a swirl of silver. Today, we're building an electric engine for an old car.

I show Doc the controller and where everything plugs into it, like Dad showed me. "Snap them into place. Never force it. Listen for the click."

Doc takes extra care—a surgeon's care—connecting the fuses and relays. It's gratifying how she takes it so seriously.

Dad would be proud.

"Lunch is ready."

I'm startled by the interruption, still not used to our party of three. Simon, our house droid, is nothing like Gage. He's purposefully plain-looking with mousy brown hair and non-descript eyes. He stands at 5-foot-8 inches and has the lanky frame of a teenager. His OS is filled with limited stats about Doc and me—like our food preferences and how we like our towels folded. He cannot acknowledge emotions nor have any. He's not programmed for intimacy to be a droid-partner. But something about his voice is familiar and catches me off-guard. Apparently, there are few options for droid vocal variations.

"Be right there, Simon," I say. "Thank you."

As he retreats into the house, Doc snickers. "You don't have to thank him, you know."

I roll my eyes. "I know. It's a habit."

Her eyebrows go up, Lederhorn-style, questioning me.

"Don't worry," I say. "I'm not going to fall in love with Simon, for crying out loud."

"Just making sure."

The grease on my hands have become part of my fingerprints, despite my efforts with the rag. I give Doc a snarky grin. "Man is his own star."

She cocks an eyebrow. "And so is woman."

Just then, my Ping flashes yellow. Simon emerges again.

"New message from headquarters."

A message from headquarters will be from Flower, who checks in on us from time to time. But why the yellow alert?

"Go ahead, Simon," Doc says. "Read it to us."

With his robot voice, Simon reports: "Your location has been identified. Not even the fiercest hounds can save you now."

Doc goes pale as her arms drop to her sides. "Hounds?"

My laugh is pure nerves. "What—is this some kind of joke?"

Simon, objective as plywood, goes inside. We follow him into the kitchen.

"Headquarters sent this?" Doc says. "Read it again."

He does, in monotone. Then, he adds: "There's a salutation."

Tension fills my body in an ugly, familiar way. In my mind, I'm already running. "What does it say? Who's it from?"

Simon sets a platter on the table; it's filled with hard cheeses and grain breads. His even tone sounds impassive, like a shrug. "It says 'the good guys.'"

I've lost my appetite. My voice shakes. "'Horosho' means 'good' in Russian."

Doc turns to me, wide-eyed. "We need to get in touch with Flower, immediately. They've been hacked. And we're in danger."

ACKNOWLEDGEMENTS

To have a team of professionals dedicated to publish your made-up story is the best compliment and ultimate validation. Thank you Immortal Works Press, including Holli, Jason, Staci, Bridget, Ashley, Jared, and everyone else, including the awesome band of authors in the IW catalogue who cheer each other on.

I'm blessed to have such supportive parental units, Jim and Janet Davies, my mother-in-law, Judith Basile, and the late Michael A. Spero.

This book would not exist if it weren't for my brilliant and inspiring husband, Anthony, who unknowingly gave me the idea after his company was hit by a Ransomware attack in February 2021. While working 24/7 to retrieve precious data without paying the $5.5 mil demand, he made the comment, "It's uncanny how similar this computer virus is to the pandemic." And the story popped into my brain like a bolt of lightning. As always, Anthony was my first reader, and the book kept him company on a business trip, making a 2-hour tarmac delay not only tolerable, but enjoyable (kind of). He came home and exclaimed, "It's your best book yet!" I love you, honey.

I owe a huge debt of gratitude to my brother, Dr. Jim Davies, full professor of Cognitive Science at Carleton University in Ottawa, Ontario. A huge SciFi fan and accomplished author himself, his feedback on my first draft informed many a revision, including the addition of several key scenes. Our talks are often about all things writing, which I cherish to no end. Of all my stories, this has the most Jimmy-influence…and is so much better for it. Love and hugs to Vanessa, my sis-in-law.

Last but not least, my boys, AJ, Adam, and Chaz, whose bookshelf is jam-packed with fantasy and dystopian series—one in particular inspired an aspect of this book. It will be an honor to see Hack Ware as part of their collection. Hopefully, a favorite!

ABOUT THE AUTHOR

JD (Johannah Davies) Spero's writing career took off when her first release, *Catcher's Keeper*, was a finalist in the Amazon Breakthrough Novel Award in 2013. Her small-town mystery series, *Boy on Hold*, has won similar acclaim—IPPY Gold for Best Mystery/Thriller. Check out her bestselling romantic suspense, *The Secret Cure,* and her newest release, *The Muse Next Door*. Having lived in various cities from St. Petersburg (Russia) to Boston, she now lives with her family in the Lake George, NY region where she was born and raised.

This has been an
Immortal Production